A Bigfoot's Quest

Becoming Alice, Book Two

Mel Braxton

A Bigfoot's Quest

Becoming Alice, Book Two

Through months of hard work, Alice has learned to be both human and Bigfoot. She's ready for rest, and spring break has arrived!

Then Jaria changes everything. She has new information on Alice's lost ma—and she is a Bigfoot in captivity! Alice and Jaria must work together to save her, all while risking their own discovery.

Only nothing matches their expectations. Soon, they are left with more questions than answers.

All Alice wants is the truth. As she shifts between her human and Bigfoot bodies, it's up to her to discover who she truly is.

for the curious

Chapter 1

"Hey, Alice," Payton said, sitting beside me on the gymnasium's bleachers. "I won't be able to make it to the movie tonight."

It was the Friday morning before spring break, and the gym buzzed with excitement. Everyone was eager for a week away from classes.

I held back my sigh of disappointment. This wasn't the first time Payton had canceled our plans, and I could already guess the reason. It'd be the same one it was every time.

"Got to work?" I asked.

She nodded. "Mom needs me to fill in the afternoon shift."

Ever since Payton started working at the Fresher Food Market, it had become more difficult for us to hang out.

"It'll be fine," I said. This change of plans was already annoying her, and hopefully my frustration didn't show. "We have all next week to see *Goblins from Outer Space*."

"When I'm not working," she added.

"And when I'm not studying."

The movie was the only thing we had prioritized over spring break. We hadn't bothered making many plans. Both of us would be too busy.

Payton had started working at the market's bakery, hoping that a little more money meant going to the movies a little more often. Since her mom was a manager at the market, Payton was the first to hear whenever someone needed their shift covered. And when one of her coworkers had asked to take spring break off, Payton had leaped at the chance to pick up extra hours.

I'd be busy too. Jaria told me I'd be doing something big for the Fae this week. But when I asked for more information, she'd refused to say more. Presumably, I'd be told to read the stack of biographies piling up on my desk.

My life as a teenage-Bigfoot-who-appears-human had been surprisingly tame for months now. It had become routine. Possibly even boring.

I spent my weekdays in Piner where my time was split between school, studying, and hanging out with Payton. My evenings were spent in the house Jaria had built with magic.

Not only did Jaria insist I have top grades, but that I continue adding information to the Fae's collective knowledge, an ethereal database available to both of us through our crystal pendants.

Access to that knowledge had become critical as I entered human society last fall. As a Bigfoot, I had never given a thought to things like t-shirts, calculators, or volleyballs. I had never read a book. It was only thanks to the Fae's knowledge that I could act somewhat normal.

Adding information to their collection had become one of my responsibilities. And despite my insistence that movies counted as cultural exposure, Jaria gave me bulky nonfiction books covering topics like history, futurism, or political theory.

Every single one of them was less exciting than a movie.

My weekends were reserved for the Bigfoot Village. At least, that had been my plan. Those days should have felt liberating. They were my days to stay in my Bigfoot skin, to be with my people.

However, during the cold winter months, I had started retreating to Jaria's house, where I could eat human food and watch more movies. Sometimes, if Payton was free, I'd go into Piner so we could hang out.

The whole thing added to my guilt. But while I understood it was important to spend time in the Bigfoot Village... I just didn't want to. At least, not anymore.

By accepting my role as a human, I'd rejected my suitorship with Daylen. He was well-liked by my Bigfoot peers, and no one could understand why I'd refused him. Between that and my mysterious role as an apprentice to the Mother, I'd become an outcast.

So really, there wasn't much for me to do in the Bigfoot Village. I only had my family—Pa, Stepma, and Bryson—and Jaria.

Not that Jaria and I were friends. Housemates? Yes. But since the Fae wouldn't talk to me directly, Jaria spoke for them, relaying their instructions. In the end, I'd decided to call Jaria my coworker.

"I'm still looking forward to next week," Payton said. "It'll be nice to do something different from school."

I nodded, glanced at the clock, and stood up. "Homeroom?"

"The bell hasn't even rung yet," she complained. "But you're wanting to see *him,* aren't you?"

I bit my lip, giving myself away. She was right.

Homeroom was the one class I shared with Mark.

"You're thinking of him again!" Payton accused.

"Am not." And yet I flushed.

Payton laughed, rising to her feet.

During the fall, Mark and I had sometimes found each other in the forest beyond the Bigfoot Village. I had liked him since the first time I'd seen him, and time had transformed that camaraderie into a crush.

But I hadn't seen him in the forest since the Winter Solstice. On that day, he'd been playing ukulele—beautifully framed as the snow fell around him. His voice had been trembling but earnest in his presumed isolation.

On that day, I'd approached him, walking silently as Bigfoots can. But when he struck a wrong chord, he cursed himself and walked away, never realizing I was there.

I longed to hear him play again, but he never returned.

It was exhausting, liking him as much as I did. I longed for him whenever we were apart—and considering we only had homeroom together, that was most of the time.

Despite the depth of my crush, I couldn't even consider a relationship with him. He was human, and I was Bigfoot. How could that ever work out? Okay, sometimes it worked out in the movies. This was real.

Mark didn't really know a single thing about me. How could he ever return my feelings if he didn't know who I was?

Payton was the only human who knew I was Bigfoot, and while I longed to tell Mark, I didn't dare. Since childhood, I'd been taught that humans were dangerous, that they were the reason my ma had vanished. Pa told me that Bigfoots needed to walk silently and hide.

"Let's go, lover girl," Payton teased, leading me from the gym.

"Hey, Payton!" someone called after us.

We turned around to find Lexi surrounded by her usual posse. She still blamed me for the team's loss in the volleyball championship, but because I was still a valuable player, most of the team liked me. That meant Lexi took out her frustration on Payton.

Lexi sneered at Payton. "Nice shirt."

It was one of her work T-shirts, emblazoned with donuts and croissants on the front and the words *'Fresher foods since 1992'* on the back.

"Is that your work uniform?" Lexi asked. "I understand if you can't train with the volleyball club in the off-season, but certainly you can afford to own different shirts for work and school."

"It's more convenient—" Payton began. "My shift starts after school—"

Lexi talked over her, "Well, don't work all break. I'd hate to think you didn't have any time for fun. Bye-bye." She turned, retreating to her giggling friends before Payton could respond.

Payton clenched her fist around the strap of her backpack and turned to the stairs. I chased after her, but no matter how many ways I said, "Lexi's just being nasty," Payton's mood stayed sour.

When I reached homeroom, I discovered Mark was already in the classroom, reading a book. He looked up as I claimed the desk next to him.

"Excited for the break?" he asked.

"Yes," I squeaked, trying to sound casual.

"Any plans?"

"I'll be with my family most of the week," I said. As far as anybody knew, my family was reclusive and

13

lived far outside of town. The story was that I had been homeschooled until my godparents sent me to high-school that fall. "But I'll be in town sometime. Payton and I want to see *Goblins from Outer Space*."

"You guys want to see that? It looks campy."

I laughed. "Exactly. We're super excited."

He shrugged, showing his disinterest. I deflated. Apparently, Mark and I didn't share movie tastes.

"If you don't watch campy movies—the best movies in existence—what do you like?" I asked.

The bell ran before he could respond.

Coach Higgins called for silence and began attendance. She turned off the lights, started the projector, and pressed play on the morning announcements.

The broadcast club had collaborated with the comedy club to make a cheesy video about spring break. It was probably entertaining, but I wanted to talk with Mark.

The video went on forever. I tapped my fingers on the desk and stole secret glances at Mark but couldn't do anything. Coach Higgins wouldn't stand any interruptions. Homeroom was nearly over, the video was still playing, and the bell would ring any moment—

"Psst."

I turned to look at Mark. His bright blue eyes flashed as he tilted his head toward the aisle between our desks. He was holding a piece of paper.

He shook it, silently asking me to take it.

I reached for it without shifting my body. Even though I was on the volleyball team, Coach Higgins wouldn't hesitate to throw the note in the trash—or worse, read it aloud—if she caught us.

I swiped the note from his hand, careful that my

finger brushed against his, and was rewarded with a jolt of his electrifying touch.

Clutching the perfect piece of paper between my fingers, I brought the note to my lap. I glanced up. Coach Higgins was looking my way, seemingly suspicious.

The bell rang.

Mark stood up, smiled, and blushed. Then he walked away like he couldn't get away fast enough.

Confused, I looked down at the note in my hand. He had written it in his beautiful, meticulous handwriting:

> Dear Alice,
>
> The thought of not seeing you next week fills me with melancholy. I was planning to ask you on a date, but this video keeps playing.
>
> So, let's make this interesting. Friday, sunset. I'll wait for you in the forest, at the place where we first met.
>
> If you say yes, I'll see you there. If not, I'll just pretend this note never reached you.
>
> Mark

I squealed and, pulling the paper to my chest, leaped to my toes.

Chasing after Mark, I ran into the hall. I hated the idea of leaving his question unanswered. *Yes, I'll be there,* I longed to say it, but he was gone. Mark had disappeared into the crowded hallway.

Chapter 2

The last bell of the day rang, and I scampered to the lawn in front of the school, claiming the bench below a maple tree. It made for the perfect vantage point, and I scanned the swarm of students scurrying from the building, searching for Mark.

Not that I knew what I would say if I found him. After carrying the weight of his note all day, I'd grown hesitant. I enjoyed being near him, and dang, I was crushing on him so hard. But he liked Alice Turner, and she wasn't really me.

"Alice!" someone called. It sounded like Jaria.

I looked around, surprised to find the Godparent Express parked at the front of the pickup queue. To have a spot like that, Jaria must have arrived early.

The car was older and seemingly not that impressive, but it was enchanted. A mannequin named Flora drove the car, acting as my legal guardian and chauffeur.

Payton had nicknamed it the Godparent Express, naming it after my 'Faery Godparents' who had orchestrated my transition into humanity. Truthfully, Jaria had done most of the work. As she said, it was part of her job as the Fae's intermediary.

My job was to be a student. To study humans so exhaustively that I could pass as one of them. Jaria followed that instruction to the letter—she had watched when Lexi gave me a bloody nose last fall, claiming it had been a human experience.

Thinking about that day still made me angry. And not at Lexi—her memory had been wiped of the experience. No, I was angry with Jaria. She'd been there the whole time, but only intervened once Lexi pulled my crystal from my chest, forcing me into my Bigfoot form.

I had just reached the Godparent Express when someone pulled my arm. Payton stood behind me.

"I've been looking for you," I said. "Something happened in homeroom—"

"Alice! Let's go!" Jaria shouted, invisible and presumably in the back seat of the car.

"Come on, Jaria," Payton said. "Give Alice a minute. It can't be that important."

The Godparent Express revved its reply.

I sighed, suddenly uninterested in talking about Mark's note now that I knew Jaria was there. "I'll tell you later. Thursday, right?"

"That's the plan," Payton agreed. "I'm looking forward to it. Have a wonderful break—you too, Jaria."

Jaria didn't reply. She never did, preferring to pretend Payton couldn't know of her existence. This was becoming a familiar game: Payton would say hi, Jaria ignored her, and Payton kept trying.

I buckled myself into the passenger seat, and Flora began driving.

"How was your day?" Jaria asked.

I thought of Mark's note in my pocket. "Pretty normal. Everyone's super excited about spring break."

"Good, good," Jaria said, her tone disinterested.

17

I looked at the back seat. It was covered with herbs, shiny stones, and several decks of cards.

"Sorry to rush you," Jaria continued. "I finished collecting my supplies and need to return to the house." Presumably she needed to cast a time-sensitive spell, but she didn't elaborate, and I knew better than to pry.

Clearly, Jaria enjoyed keeping information from me, and I refused to give her the satisfaction of knowing how badly it irked me.

We rode in silence, crossing the small downtown district and the Fresher Food Market before turning onto the highway. We passed the town's exit sign, *Thanks for visiting Piner. Enjoy the mountains.*

I wasn't exactly sure when Jaria and I agreed to talk only when necessary, but our pact had been mutual.

Ever since the incident with Lexi, I couldn't trust her. She was angry that I'd told Payton everything and wouldn't trust me either. Regardless, we had to work together, and awkward silences were better than fighting.

I changed the radio station and stared out the window. It seemed ridiculous to call this week spring break—the trees seemed too bare for that. The earth was damp with constant rains, and while the snow on Northridge had finally melted... Spring had not yet sprung, and I was tense with anticipation.

We didn't speak until the car turned from the highway and began plodding up the wiggly, narrow road that weaved deeper into the forest.

"I told you something big was going to happen this week," Jaria began.

"Yeah?" I tried not to sound too interested.

"We're going to find your ma."

My stomach lurched. That was not what I expected. For the first time all day, I forgot about Mark's note.

"The Fae want to speak with her, and we're responsible for bringing her back to the village," she continued, as if her pronouncement wouldn't have a tremendous impact on me. "It's taken me months to research and prepare everything, but we'll be ready to leave on Monday."

I swallowed, calming my thudding heart. My ma. Jaria's secretive spring break plans involved finding my long-lost mother? I gaped.

Maybe I shouldn't have been so surprised—Jaria told me my ma was alive last fall—but I didn't dare believe she was telling the truth. Jaria never brought it up again, and it was too much to wish for.

She seemed serious now.

"I can see my ma?" I asked.

"Didn't I say we need to bring her back to the village? That means you'll see her."

Hope fluttered in my chest, but I worked to beat it down, fearing disappointment. But—maybe this was happening. Jaria lied through deception and omission, but she'd said this plainly. This could be real.

I had watched my ma cross the boundary that final time when I was a child, not much older than my half-brother was now. My memories of that day were foggy and warped by the years, but once I'd believed she'd return.

Back then, Pa told me that the humans had taken her, and we had performed the burial rites without a body. Still, I refused to believe she was dead. My denial stemmed from a naïve and childish hope, one I thought Jaria was manipulating.

But now, considering everything I knew about the Fae and the power of the crystal pendant, the same type of pendant my ma had once worn... anything seemed possible.

"Tell me your plan," I said.

"Come to the house on Sunday at sunrise. I'll explain more then. Tell your family not to expect you back until Monday night."

"It's an overnight adventure?" I asked. Even if I spent all my days between Piner and Jaria's house, I always returned to my family's cabin to sleep.

She repeated herself, "You won't be back until Monday."

Her answer gave me no more information, but if I asked again, it'd be a waste of words. Instead, I sat on my hands to keep them from twitching. I swayed in my seat with uncontained excitement. We were going to rescue my ma.

Chapter 3

As soon as we reached the house, I dropped my backpack at my desk and scampered back outside.

Knowing Jaria's agenda changed everything.

The same weather that had seemed so oppressive during the car ride felt transformed. The earth remained damp, but at least the rain had stopped. Trees were still bare, but now the birds sang.

There was the promise of adventure—a quest that would bring my ma home—and the thrill of it lightened my steps.

I walked with purpose, quickly reaching the boundary of the Bigfoot lands. Without pausing, I marched across the glittering golden perimeter, transforming into my Bigfoot form.

My heart skipped in my chest. Thrilled by the sensation, I began to run, following the trail that lined the boundary. It was rarely used, making it perfect for an afternoon jog. I found a tempo in my legs and settled into a comfortable pace. My feet pounded against the dirt. My mood couldn't be better—

Two Bigfoots were walking on the path ahead. Daylen and Heron. I did a double-take and stumbled, catching myself awkwardly.

Since ending our suitorship, I preferred to avoid Daylen. It wasn't that I didn't want to talk to him, but

21

that I had to swallow a knot of jealousy every time I looked at him. Our banter still came easily, and every time we did talk, I was reminded how wonderful our relationship had been, how delicious his kisses had been. Our suitorship was one of many things I'd surrendered to embrace my human identity.

"Just passing through." I forced myself to jog further down the path, closing the distance between us.

Daylen was carrying a game sack, possibly one we had once carried when we had trapped together, with a sheathed knife at his waist. Heron held a spear.

"Hey, Alice," Daylen said. "We're checking the traps."

Heron didn't seem happy to see me, and his face scrunched as I approached. "Your work for the Mother takes you far from home," he observed.

"I'm out for a run." I slowed to a walk beside them.

"What is it that drives you and Jaria to the outskirts of the Bigfoot land?" Heron frowned. "The other females are busy with their trades, and you two are—what—tramping around the forest? Do you tell each other scary human stories and play at magic?" He laughed.

Daylen didn't laugh with him, but he knew the truth of my apprentice. I dared to glance at him, finding his expression stony and cold.

"You're just still angry that Jaria refused your kiss," I said.

He shrugged. "She shouldn't have embarrassed me so publicly."

"And you shouldn't kiss people who don't want to be kissed," I accused. "I wouldn't be surprised if she put toads in your bed after that."

Daylen surprised me by laughing. Maybe Jaria

22

really had put toads in Heron's bed. Or snakes.

Heron's expression sharpened. "But if I somehow become Jaria's suitor, I'd keep better hold of her—better than Daylen did with you."

Daylen's laughter stalled, his expression becoming inscrutable.

But Heron continued, "You apprentices to the Mother think you're so different, lingering in strange parts of our lands. But the hunters are the ones who protect you from bears and mountain lions!" He shoved his spear into the air, waving it like it gave him authority.

And maybe it did represent power. Hunting was an esteemed trade for Bigfoot males. I should know; Pa was their leader, and I'd been raised in the shadow of his honor. But after living as a human for months—learning of their war machines—I wasn't as impressed by the spear as I used to be.

He waved it in the air a second time.

And I leaped forward to take it.

Either I moved fast or caught him by surprise—either way, I snagged the spear from his grasp.

With his spear in my hand, I began running again. I laughed, howling with derision. Pa would be upset with me when he found out—

—*slam*—

Someone tripped my leg, and I tumbled to the ground.

"Don't go running with weapons." Heron plucked the spear from my grasp. He held it over me, and I snarled at him.

"Stop it," Daylen shouted, pulling at Heron's other arm.

Heron growled, but stepped back. "I'll never understand why you defend her."

I stood up and looked at Daylen. "Thank you."

He turned away, speaking to Heron. "Let's get back to work."

They walked away, and I continued my run. But soon I slowed, twisting around to sneak a final glance at Daylen, hoping he might glance at me too.

He didn't.

Dinner was a typical affair. Stepma had brought home a pot of stew and a loaf of bread from the cookhouse. She'd stored them on the stove to keep warm.

While stoves kept the Bigfoot cabins warm, they weren't used for cooking. It was one of the many things that I'd never considered before starting high school. But lately, the lack of a stove seemed like a limitation. And it wasn't the only one. I'd also grown accustomed to the luxury of having a fridge, running water, and a microwave.

I served the stew into the bowls as Bryson broke the loaf into pieces. We crowded around the small table in the dim candlelight.

No electronics beeped around us. Instead, I heard the sounds of the forest and the hum of the village. These quiet hours with my family could be peaceful and divine; they could be irritatingly quiet.

Bryson talked most of dinner. He had thought of some new questions during the day. Why is the ocean so big? Why are the stars like the sun? But most importantly, he wanted to know tomorrow's weather: when would the rainy season end? Every day he had new questions to ask, and for a little while, I enjoyed indulging him with those tidbits of information I could provide.

Bryson's ability to keep my secret impressed me. Stepma said his new knowledge was starting to confuse the other kids, possibly alienating him, but he never explained where he'd gotten his information.

Stepma and Pa had grown accustomed to my new position. Fortunately, my role as the Mother's apprentice was an honored one, even if it was isolating.

Pa clearly wished I'd chosen Daylen over these abilities, but he didn't argue about it. As for Stepma, she revered the Fae and was thankful I did their work.

"Jaria has something planned next week," I blurted out as we reached the end of our dinner. "She says I won't be here Sunday night."

Pa frowned, but Stepma said, "If that's what the Fae need."

"It is." I hesitated and considered telling them everything—that we were going to bring my ma home—but decided against it. I had not told them that she was alive, and I couldn't say the words now. Maybe fear stopped me. Not only the fear that I'd fail...

I was afraid of how this would change my family.

Yes, I was thrilled to see my ma, but I couldn't imagine bringing her back to my family—her *former* family. I liked Stepma, loved her and Bryson both. What would Evie's return mean for them? What would Pa do? Nothing like this had ever happened before. The Council would have to get involved and... and...

My stomach twisted. What if my family couldn't stay together? No, I couldn't tell them about it.

"Since you'll be gone on Sunday, can we play tomorrow?" Bryson asked. "I've got so many ideas!" There was a whine in his voice, the sound tugging at my heartstrings.

"Of course," I said, though it was likely a lie.

I'd said the same thing every single weekend for months, but the words hadn't changed my behavior. Most likely, I'd slip out of the cabin the moment I woke up. I'd go to the house and watch more movies, cook frozen pizzas, and eat ice cream.

Bryson stared at me and blinked his big brown eyes. He'd felt the lie too. His downcast expression made me wish he'd confront me, yell at me, and even demand that I explain why I didn't play anymore. I wish he would call me what I was: a rotten sister.

But even if he asked, I didn't know my answer. Playing with him wasn't as exciting as it used to be. Maybe I'd simply grown out of the games. Maybe I was becoming too human.

"Okay," he said aloud.

Stepma considered the space between me and Bryson, tapping her fingers. Then she stood and brought the dice to the table. "How about you two help me clear the table, and then we can play games?"

Late that evening, I crawled into the loft Bryson and I shared for a bedroom. Bryson had been sent to bed while the rest of us played a more complex game with tokens like human dominos.

I was settling in my cot when I heard someone climbing the ladder. Stepma sat down in the gap between Bryson's bed and mine.

"Is everything okay with you and Bryson?" she asked.

I looked away. "I love him so much, but…"

She waited, refusing to let it go.

I sighed. "I don't know. I just—I can't."

The silence dragged out.

"And there's no need to reprimand me for it," I continued. "I realize I'm being an awful sister, and trust me, I feel horrible about it." I thought of my ma, knowing I wasn't only a bad sister, but a terrible daughter too.

"What if playing together isn't what you want anymore? Maybe there are other activities you can share."

She had a point. "Do you have any ideas?" I asked.

"He's really obsessed with your human stories."

I shook my head. "He shouldn't be interested in that."

"Why not?"

"It's not… Bigfoot. And it's already separating him from his friends. What's the point? He'll never even see a human."

Stepma shrugged, implying it didn't matter. I shook my head, frustrated she wasn't as concerned as me.

Eager to change the subject, I reached under my pillow and pulled Mark's note from where I'd hidden it. "Mark wants to meet me." I continued by reading his message aloud.

"This is what you wanted, isn't it?" she asked.

"I guess so."

She waited.

I continued, "I'm not comfortable telling him what I am."

"That's okay," she replied. "You don't need to tell

him."

"But how can anything work between us? Everything about me is a lie."

"But you still act like you, don't you?"

I shrugged, unconvinced.

Stepma sighed. "Give it time. You said humans go on these dates without committing to relationships. All he wants is a date, right?"

I nodded.

"Then go on the date and see what happens. You've learned how to blend in, and I have faith you can understand this problem too."

Stepma had too much faith in me, but I didn't feel like protesting. She pulled me into a hug, and I relaxed in her warmth, her familiar smell. And despite my rising fear, the worry that searching for my ma meant betraying her, she comforted me.

Chapter 4

Bryson woke when I stirred on Sunday morning. He watched me with one sleepy eye as I brushed my fur.

"Are you leaving?" he asked.

"I need to meet Jaria at sunrise."

"You'll be back tomorrow?"

"Mmhmm."

He rolled to his side, facing the wall instead of me. I reached to him, but stopped, my hand hovering over his shoulder.

I'd spent a few hours with him yesterday, but it wasn't enough. When I woke on Saturday morning, he was still asleep. As expected, I'd gone to the house, telling myself I'd return to him early...

But then it was lunchtime, and I wanted to eat human food. And during the afternoon, there was a movie I wanted to finish.

I didn't end up coming home until late afternoon. Sure, I'd immediately joined him—we ran to the river and ran its shore, pushing each other into the water— but soon we had to return home for dinner, and he threw a fit when I said we had to turn around.

I didn't stop him. Instead, I'd let him exhaust himself with his tantrum. I understood why he was angry at me and let him yell, believing it was what I deserved.

Despite how frustrated both of us had become, I was enchanted by my human life and leaving Bryson behind.

Still wrapped in his blanket, he stared at the wall. I finally touched his shoulder and was relieved that he turned my way. I gave him my prettiest smile.

"I'll tell you something," I began. "Jaria and I are going on an adventure."

"What sort of adventure?"

"The type that'll make the best story. I'll tell you more when I get back. I know you like my stories."

He considered me for a long moment. "Really?" he asked.

"Yes."

He nodded, his eyes shifting again. I leaned forward and kissed his forehead.

"Now go back to sleep." I climbed down from the loft.

Pa sat in his usual chair, eating his usual jerky and nuts. A morning routine. I grabbed my breakfast, poured a glass of water, and sat down next to him.

We didn't talk, only grunting as we ate, like always. There was ease in our custom.

I still hadn't told him that if everything went well, I'd be returning with my ma. The omission was not from fear but doubt. Without knowing more about Jaria's plan, the objective seemed impossible. My memories of my ma were like a distant dream, and no matter how hard I tried, I couldn't picture her in my reality.

I gulped the last of my water. "I'll see you tomorrow?"

"Tomorrow. Stay safe and come back soon." His brows were creased. He was focused—or worried.

I kissed him goodbye and skipped out of the cabin. I began my morning run, traveling beyond the village. Soon I passed through the frosty, bare farmlands that surrounded the village, crossing into the surrounding forest. I ran farther, deeper into the trees until I reached the perimeter and the fallen tree I had once called mine, that Ma had called hers.

I jumped onto its trunk and used the height to leap across the glinting golden boundary. I transformed in the air, landing as a human on the other side. I'd practiced the jump many times, hoping it looked as cool as I imagined.

I ran past the spot where I met Mark and squirmed with excitement. Soon. But not soon enough. Even if I was nervous, I still couldn't wait to see him on Friday.

I jumped across the stream and reached the house. By human standards, it wasn't much, but it was huge compared to the cabin I shared with my family.

When Jaria had first brought me to the house, I'd been more confused than impressed. By now, between long evenings doing homework and weekends watching movies, I'd realized how much forethought Jaria had shown when she'd built it.

I touched the doorknob, and it warmed to my touch before unlocking. Like many things in the house, it was enchanted. Only Jaria or I could set foot inside the house. While we could theoretically invite guests, that hadn't happened.

I turned on a lamp. My backpack peeked from behind the desk where I'd shoved it on Friday. My laptop and phone charged on the desk, tucked between stacks of thick, boring nonfiction books.

Food wrappers and empty soda cans covered the

coffee table. The couch cushions were barely visible under the piles of blankets that made my movie-watching nest. The kitchen was as messy as the rest of the house, but it was Jaria's turn to do the dishes. We'd discussed that yesterday...

I removed my pendant, relieved to return to my Bigfoot form, and wrapped the cord of the necklace around my wrist.

While Jaria had finished the house in the summer, she couldn't finish all the enchantments until the Winter Solstice... something about correspondences and harnessing the right energies. Now, not only were the doorknobs enchanted, but the windows too. No one could see that Bigfoots lived in this house.

I tiptoed up the staircase and peeked into the loft. Jaria's bed was unmade, but presumably she was still in the house. The bathroom door was closed.

Jaria was the seventh child of ten and wasn't close with her family. While her apprenticeship had awarded her honor and respect, it also emphasized her strangeness, straining an already feeble relationship with her family. After living with the Fae for two years, Jaria had stayed with Mother Gazina. Now that the house was fully enchanted, it was where she usually lived.

I still didn't know much about her time with the Fae. She avoided my questions, and I'd stopped asking.

Jaria stepped from the bathroom. "Good, you're here. We can get started."

"Get started on what, exactly?" I asked.

She pointed toward the center of the living area. "We'll need some space to work. Can you move the coffee table out of the way? I'll prepare my supplies."

I didn't understand what she had planned, but I cleared the rubbish from the table and pushed it against a wall.

Meanwhile, Jaria inspected her closet. She retrieved several candles, a lighter, a knife, a ball of yarn, and a circular piece of paper with an intricate symbol drawn onto it.

"Stand there." She pointed to the center of the space. "I'll need you to hold really still while I cast the spell. It might take a little while, so make sure you're comfortable."

I did as she requested.

"You need to transform into your human form. And don't change back! Shifting will break my spell."

"Okay," I said, considering her request. I'd never spent more than a day in my human body. "Can you please tell me what we're doing?"

"Making you persuasive," she said absently, cutting two holes at opposite ends of the circular paper. "So persuasive that anyone will do what you say, even when your request doesn't make sense."

"Would it hurt if you explained a little more? Like, how will being persuasive help us rescue my ma?"

Jaria measured out an arm's length of yarn and cut it. "I know where she is, but I need your help reaching her. Invisibility can only take me so far."

"Where is she?"

Jaria continued her work, tying the yarn into one of the holes in the paper. "Aldertown," she said finally.

I knew of Aldertown but had never visited. Payton's father lived there with her step-family, and she had visited them over the winter holidays. If my memory was accurate, the drive took half a day.

Jaria stepped closer to me and tutted, pointing to

my pendant. I took her hint and put it on, transforming my body into that of a human.

She wrapped her arms around me, almost like a hug, and tightened the yarn at my waist. Then she tied the other end into the second hole, modifying the paper's placement until it was securely centered over my bellybutton.

Nodding, she stepped back and appreciated her work. "More specifically, she's at the Supernatural Entities Agency."

"The what?"

"SEA. They have an office in Aldertown, not far from the university."

The Supernatural Entities Agency. I watched enough TV to know that didn't sound good. "Why would she be there?" I shuddered. "Did they... capture her?"

Jaria pinched me. "Hold still." She sighed. "Alice, I don't know."

"What *do* you know?"

"Last fall, the Fae told me two things. First, they knew your ma—Evie—was alive. Second, they told me Evie's last known location. They asked me to find out where she'd gone. For the last few months, I've been following her trail. It's nearly a decade old and difficult to follow... but I'm sure it leads to SEA."

"You've been there?"

She nodded. "It's fenced in, and I can't cross the perimeter. Like the house, it's enchanted." She shook her head, clearly annoyed by this obstacle. "But there's a gate, one for cars. If you can convince them to let us inside, I'll be able to continue my search."

I swallowed, taking in her words. So she wanted us—two Bigfoots—to drive up to a property owned by the Supernatural Entities Agency, a group who already held one Bigfoot captive.

"We need more information," I concluded.

"I've done what I can without you. The Fae say they've worked with SEA before, and they're the ones who recommended this plan."

I didn't find that particularly reassuring.

Jaria must have seen my hesitation. She rested her fur-covered hand on my lanky shoulder. "It's for Evie, okay?"

I chewed my lip. When my ma had vanished, Jaria had grieved beside me. While I refused to trust Jaria completely, I knew she cared for my ma. "For Evie," I agreed.

"Good." She began arranging the four candles, placing them in a square around me in what I thought were the four cardinal directions. "This persuasion spell should do the trick. If I do this right, a sigil like the one I drew on the paper will form on your stomach. The spell will take time to set, and the sigil won't appear until tomorrow's sunrise. Now hold still."

She lit the north-facing candle, and I sneezed.

Jaria continued to work around me, lighting the candles one by one. While I understood Jaria had become some sort of magic-wielding Fae-communicating Bigfoot-witch, I had not witnessed many active spells.

Spells like my pendant or the house were already cast, set into objects, and the spellwork had become passive. But active spells were those in the process of forming and were far more sensitive to intention and environment. Active spells bothered me in the same way the boundary-creating Crux did, and I avoided them.

This was only the second time I'd been in the

presence of Jaria's spellcasting. The first being when she'd wiped Lexi's memory.

I sneezed again, and she glared at me. "Careful. Don't ruin the spell."

"What should I be doing? I'm just supposed to stand here?"

"Basically." She considered. "But it wouldn't hurt if you thought persuasive ideas? I'm sure adding your intention can only improve the spell."

I rolled my eyes but held in a third sneeze. And... I began wondering about persuasion. This mission was much more important than some petty fight between Jaria and myself. Both of us wanted Evie returned.

Persuasion. I had to persuade SEA to let me see their Bigfoot. My strongest power would lie in my words.

My words would save my ma from SEA.

But even as I thought about it, repeating the phrases, I questioned. We didn't know SEA's intentions or abilities. Jaria didn't know how they had even taken my ma. Maybe the Fae approved this plan, but that didn't make me feel safe.

Yet as Jaria chanted, using a language I'd never heard before, I fell into the rhythm of her sounds. I let my awareness bleed, surrendered myself around a single thought: if words could reconnect me with my ma, I would say the most persuasive things.

Chapter 5

I woke Monday morning with an unbearable itch on my belly. Closing my eyes, I tried to go back to sleep, but the itchiness was growing unbearable.

Surrendering, I scratched at my abdomen, my fingers running over something textured. The sigil. Scratching couldn't be good for it. I pulled my fingers away and rolled over. I closed my eyes, willing sleep to return, but the skin on my belly continued to complain.

Sighing, I stretched out, enjoying how luxuriously large this bed was compared to the cot I used in my family's cabin. Turning to my side, I saw Jaria was still fast asleep. After only one night here, I understood exactly why she'd made this house her home.

I walked down the stairs from the bedroom loft, catching my reflection in the tall mirror next to the door. I'd never slept in my human body before and was horrified to discover my hair was a mess. My short brown locks spiked in strange directions, and my clothes were wrinkled from sleeping in them.

I frowned and checked the closet, relieved it was stocked with a few outfits—typically, I put on a new outfit through transformation. Today, I took clothes with me into the bathroom.

Attempting to tame my hair with water, I studied

my face in the mirror. Between my two appearances, my deep brown eyes were the most similar. Otherwise, my human face appeared too angular, and, with no fur to bulk up my body, I looked too lanky, too small.

Of course, I wasn't actually small. I was unusually tall for a woman and towered over my classmates, even the boys. Curiously, I was the same height both as a Bigfoot and a human—Payton and I had determined that one rainy Saturday afternoon. It seemed that the magic inside my pendent only transformed my appearance as much as necessary.

I removed my slept-in shirt and examined my itchy, inflamed tummy. Like a tattoo, the symbol from the paper had been etched onto my skin.

As Jaria had promised, it must have materialized sometime around sunrise. It should have been a good thing—it meant the persuasion spell had set correctly—but Jaria failed to warn me how it would make my skin blotchy and itchy.

At least I knew better than to scratch the spellwork. We needed this to last the day.

Sighing out my discomfort, I changed into my new outfit: skinny jeans, a blouse, and a jacket. The look was more mature than the simple T-shirts and zip-hoodies I wore most days. I smiled, then frowned. I pulled my lips wide, stuck out my tongue, and made a face. I laughed.

Would Ma even recognize me?

I couldn't expect her to. Not only had I been a child the last time we'd seen each other, but she'd see me as a human. It shouldn't have mattered since I could explain it to her.

Yet everything felt much more complicated than that. I wanted her to recognize me. Emotions, too tangled to unravel, tightened instead.

I stared at my reflection, trying to imagine how my ma would see me. I looked and acted human, dressed like one too. Moreover, if I could be honest with myself, my transformation was deeper than skin level—I was truly becoming one of them.

Jaria knocked at the bathroom door. "Can I get in?"

"Yeah—Sorry!" I called back, picking up my worn clothes and walking out.

She glanced at my stomach. "Did the spell set okay?" she asked.

I lifted my shirt enough to show her the mark. "I think so."

"It's so... red."

"Itches too."

"That's not normal..." She ran her finger over the symbol. "But the shape of the sigil is in good shape. It should hold until sunset."

I pulled my shirt back over my stomach. "Let me pass, and I'll go eat some breakfast."

She obeyed, instinctive and immediate. Then, realizing what had happened, her mouth gaped open. "It worked! That definitely was persuasion magic."

"Really?" I asked, realization of this superpower dawning on me. "Maybe I'll ask you to make me food. I would like—"

She slammed the bathroom door before I could continue. At first, I thought she was angry, but then I heard her giggle.

The door creaked back open. "By the way, I've found a hair product that's been working wonders on my fur. Maybe it'll help with your hair."

"I don't need—" I glanced at my reflection in the entryway mirror. My hair was sticking up again.

"Thanks. If you can leave it on the counter, that'd be great."

"No problem," she replied, closing the door again.

We worked quickly that morning, each of us keeping our thoughts private. Everything fell together so fast that I had to do a double take when Jaria donned her pendant and became invisible.

It was time to go.

Flora came to life as we loaded into the car. She turned the key and began the drive. I settled into my seat, pulling the seatbelt away from my itching stomach. Then I turned up the radio, not because I liked the music, but because I needed the noise.

Chapter 6

Hours later, distant farmhouses and scattered towns became developing neighborhoods as we reached the outskirts of Aldertown. While Piner had a population many times larger than that of the Bigfoot Village, Aldertown was even bigger than that, making it the largest city I'd ever seen.

While the sheer size of human civilization no longer overwhelmed me, it remained unfathomable. My only comfort was the growing sense that humans couldn't comprehend the extent of their society either.

Soon, we passed by a sign reading, *University of Aldertown,* and began following the campus boundary. It was the first college I'd ever seen. By listening to seniors on the volleyball team, I knew this school was a popular choice. Not that there were many schools to choose from in our part of the country.

Allegedly, the Fae wanted me to earn an advanced degree. Since the University of Aldertown was somewhat near the Bigfoot Village, I wondered if I could be a student there one day. I struggled to imagine it. Day in and day out inside my human body, always hours away from home.

My stomach itched anew at the thought.

The campus ended, backing against a tree covered hill, while the road continued onward. We drove upward, following it deeper into the forest.

A few minutes later, Flora slowed, and I wondered if we were lost. Then Flora approached a steep driveway blocked by a large, fenced gate.

"That's it, isn't it?" I asked Jaria.

"We've reached SEA," she confirmed.

My throat constricted as I saw the speaker box in front of the gate. The fence continued to both sides of the entrance, disappearing into the forest. It was made from wood planks, obstructing my view of the other side.

The fence also looked easy to climb, if it came to that. Though Jaria had said something about an enchantment...

A nearby sign warned, *Government Property, No Trespassing.* It was the single indication that this was SEA.

"Alice, it's your turn. Persuade them," Jaria said. "And mention a Dr. Oleski."

Flora parked in front of the speaker box.

"Do you have an appointment?" the speaker chirped as Flora rolled down the window.

I swallowed, cleared my throat, and said, "I'm here to speak with Dr. Oleski." The words sounded weaker than I'd hoped.

A pause. "I'm sorry, I don't see an appointment."

"Can you check with him? Tell him it's Alice." My name wouldn't mean anything. I cringed but continued, "Alice Turner. I called Dr. Oleski earlier about—about an encounter with a Bigfoot—and he recommended an in-person interview. I know this is all very last minute, but Dr. Oleski really wants to speak with me."

Another pause. This one was longer.

"Dr. Oleski says he'll meet with you."

The gate began rolling aside, and I sighed my relief. It worked! Well, at least it'd worked so far.

Flora continued up the steep driveway, turning with the switchbacks. My stomach twisted, but I didn't know if it was caused by carsickness, nerves, or the insistent itching of my belly. Despite the minutes spent climbing the hill, I failed to calm myself.

All too soon, Flora had parked in a small lot. She turned off the engine and pulled out a tabloid magazine, pretending to be completely engrossed.

With one burst of courage, I opened the door. I stood to look around, holding the door ajar for Jaria to scramble out.

The building was positioned on the hill's peak, and the forest sprawled around it. While the structure wasn't in disrepair, it was old and far more utilitarian than appealing.

However, a rooftop garden made up for its blandness. Vines ventured down from the roof, bringing life to the dull concrete exterior. Shrubs grew at the roof's edge, forming a barrier so thick I couldn't see past the greenery.

But nothing—no placard or sign—identified the building's purpose.

"SEA?" I whispered to Jaria. "Are you sure this is SEA?"

"The Fae confirmed it," Jaria said as something cold and misty passed over my hand. It was the feel of her touch—while invisible she couldn't interact with living beings—and her ghost-like contact acted as a signal. She was beside me, and it was time to go.

We walked up a quick flight and reached the building's entrance. I pulled at the door but found it locked.

"There's a doorbell," Jaria whispered. I pressed the button.

"Alice Turner?" a voice asked, the same one I had talked to at the gate.

Finding a camera near the doorbell, I smiled and waved. "I'm ready to meet with Dr. Oleski. It'd be a shame to send me away now."

I forced my mouth in to an innocent smile while I waited for a response.

The door buzzed unlocked. "Come on in."

I inhaled and stepped into a small lobby. There was a desk with a woman with graying hair behind it. "Dr. Oleski will be down shortly," she said.

An elevator opened, and a man stepped into the lobby. He was tall, angular, and carrying a notebook that he was actively writing in. He glanced up at me and nodded.

I approached him, extending my hand before I could reconsider. "I'm Alice Turner. I noticed Bigfoot activity near my family's house and was told we should discuss it in person."

We shook hands. "And I'm Dr. Oleski," he said. "You said we talked on the phone? I don't quite remember—"

"It was late last night," I improvised.

He scribbled something in his journal. "Please forgive me, umm, Miss Alice... but why did I ask you to come here?"

"You said I should meet your Bigfoot..." The lie began taking shape in my mind. "I may have seen a Bigfoot last night, and we wanted to confirm what I saw."

Dr. Oleski lifted his pen from the notebook and looked up. "That doesn't sound like something I would—"

I held his gaze, trying to make my point clear. "I may have seen multiple Bigfoots. You said this was an unusual case. I need to see the Bigfoot that is kept here."

Dr. Oleski's scrutiny fell, and he nodded. "Of course. Well then, you better follow me." He called the elevator, and the door opened.

I squared my shoulders, holding back my sigh of relief.

We stepped into the elevator, and Jaria brushed my hand, reminding me I wasn't alone. Dr. Oleski pressed the button for the fourth floor—the highest floor.

"Humor me," Dr. Oleski said as the elevator hummed. "Why is it important for you to see Evie?"

Evie. He called my ma by name.

"The Bigfoots were acting suspicious. It's possible they were planning something." I began. "And you... you thought I should talk to Evie about it."

He returned to his journal, frowned, and continued writing. It was difficult to persuade someone who wouldn't give me their full attention. I wondered if I should ask him to hand over the notebook.

He looked back up, his expression doubtful. "Did I really say that?"

"You did," I insisted, saying the words forcefully. It might have worked—he didn't ask another question.

We stepped onto the fourth floor, and he led me down the hallway. Some of the doors were open. I could see into offices, meeting rooms, and storage closets. Everything seemed so benign. There was no evidence of the dark cages I had expected.

He opened a door and stepped into a long narrow office. Bookshelves lined one wall, and a chalkboard covered the opposite one. Clutter filled the room: art, trinkets, and books. Chalk dust and random papers covered nearly every available surface.

I tried not to panic when I read the chalkboard's message: *Bigfoot culture: tribalistic, community-focused, and self-isolating.*

Regardless, goosebumps rose on my arm.

He grabbed a few books from a shelf and rejoined me in the hall. I peeked at them, but only made out a partial title: *Fae Enchantments and...* His hand blocked the rest.

"We will meet Evie now?" I asked, struggling to keep my voice confident. Something was off about this man. Something was wrong about that notebook. "It's very important for me to talk to her."

He studied me for a long second but finally began walking further down the hallway. He pointed toward a stairwell. "Let's go to the roof, shall we?"

"The roof?"

"The rooftop garden? It's where Evie lives."

Chapter 7

We climbed a flight of stairs and reached a door labeled, *Danger: Roof Access,* but Dr. Oleski didn't hesitate. He pulled a key from his pocket and unlocked the door.

I expected Evie to be in a dark cell, trapped and lonely. I believed only state-of-the-art captivity was strong enough to stand between her and me. Realizing she lived in a rooftop garden caught me completely by surprise.

The plants were carefully tended. Large evergreen hedges bordered the exterior, hiding the surrounding forest from view. Raised garden beds lined one side, lettuces and carrots growing stubbornly in the cold dirt.

A small cabin had been constructed on the roof; its architecture recognizable. It looked like the cabins in the Bigfoot Village.

Finally, my gaze landed upon *her.*

She looked our way. I gaped at the sight, hoping Dr. Oleski saw it as a normal reaction to meeting a Bigfoot. She sat in an oversized chair near a human-sized table. She set down a book, *Alice's Adventures in Wonderland.*

The book distracted me. And by the time I found the courage to face her, I had forgotten how to breathe.

My ma—Evie. She was both familiar and unknown. Her fur curled around her forehead, just as mine did, and it struck me how much I was beginning to look like her. Fragmented memories returned to me, like the way her brow furrowed when she was interrupted, like she was doing now.

When had her muzzle grown so white? I suppose Pa's had too, but it had happened so gradually...

She looked at me as I studied her, and I wished she could recognize me. But I couldn't expect her to see past the years of growth and a human disguise.

Besides, even though I could identify her face and had read her expression, I also didn't recognize her. While I understood that she was my ma, I failed to find the bubbly, playful mother from my childhood. This calm and studious Bigfoot was a stranger. This was *Evie*.

"I'm sorry for the interruption," Dr. Oleski said, waving his notebook in the air. "But this young lady needs to talk to you. She witnessed Bigfoot behavior last night."

"If I wanted to be alone, I'd be in the cabin." She grinned at him like this was an old joke, a line she had said before. Their familiarity deepened my discomfort.

"Very well," Dr. Oleski began. "This is Evie. She came to live with us... Has it been ten years?"

"A little more." She leaned back in her chair. "They've been good years, haven't they? A fortunate turn of events, all things considered."

Their easy conversation was alarming. This was not my expectation. I had believed it would take chains to keep a mother from her child—but apparently, my ma read books in a rooftop garden.

"That's a nice pendant," she said. Her expression sharpened in intensity, and she began studying me with renewed interest.

I clutched the crystal in my palm. She grew still.

"Evie, meet Alice," Dr. Oleski said.

"Alice?" she asked, her eyes widening.

I met her gaze—holding it took all my courage— and knew she understood. She knew me as her daughter. I glanced away, looking at the cover of her book. *Alice's Adventures in Wonderland.* I had always wondered why she named me *Alice.* It wasn't a Bigfoot name.

"Evie does all the gardening herself. She's wonderful, isn't she?" Dr. Oleski continued, unaware of the full nature of the introduction he was facilitating.

"You never had a green thumb before." My words sounded snippier than I intended. "I mean, I didn't realize Bigfoots had green thumbs."

"I came to it later in life." Hopefully, it was my imagination, but she began shifting uncomfortably.

"Why don't you take a seat?" Dr. Oleski said to me. "You're not the first to be intimidated when meeting Evie." He took a chair for himself and returned to his journal.

This was the first moment I had shared with Evie in years, but I couldn't tell if I wanted to hug her or yell. And I couldn't do either in Dr. Oleski's presence.

I swallowed. "Dr. Oleski, maybe I should talk with Evie alone. Can you go back to your office?"

He stood, still writing in the journal. He paused.

"And give that to me," I commanded, reaching out for the notebook. He offered it to me.

Evie snatched it first. Her eyes scanned the page, and she grinned. "Carl, you nearly outsmarted her."

He peered at her, his expression vague.

She handed the journal to me. "He wrote down everything you said. Once the spell's influence had passed, he would have deduced what you'd done." She considered me with fresh curiosity. "I thought it'd be impossible for you to use magic."

"I-I didn't cast the spell." I gaped. "Jaria—"

"Carl, can you leave us for a bit?" Evie said.

Dr. Oleski looked from Evie and back to me. "Are you sure?" While he was uncomfortable, he didn't seem disconcerted enough. Clearly, my trick was not his first exposure to magic.

"Don't worry, I'll explain soon," Evie continued.

"I'll return in fifteen minutes?" he asked.

"Sure."

He left, finally giving us the privacy to have a proper conversation. The problem was, I had no idea what to say.

Chapter 8

Even as I longed to embrace her, an uncomfortable truth held me back: Evie was practically a stranger. She seemed unsure too. Her gaze darted across my face, taking in my appearance with desperate curiosity.

I exhaled, overwhelmed by my childish daydreams, shocked by my observations of reality. "Ma?"

"Alice," she whispered.

She seemed so serious, almost sad. I looked away first, and I lifted the pendant. "The crystal makes me appear human."

"Can I... can I hug you?" she asked.

"Of course." I leaped to my feet, thankful she'd asked.

Evie needed a moment to stand. She grabbed a nearby staff and shifted her weight, using the staff to help her up.

I didn't mean to stare. But I did.

She moved so heavily, favoring her right leg far more than her left. She looked at the staff and tapped it against the rooftop. "It's an old injury. Doesn't hurt."

"It's fine."

I closed the distance between us, slowed by the

realization I was about her height. She tugged me into an embrace, and with her fur around me, I found some comfort.

She smelled of human soap scented with geraniums, not the woodsy scent I recalled. Her fur was unusually soft, and her body had shed the dense muscles necessary for life in the Bigfoot Village.

As she held me, I tried to hold on to that moment, to treasure our first hug in years. I had been looking forward to this. And yet, my mind started skipping straight to questions. My hold loosened.

Evie stepped back first, one hand still holding my shoulder. She examined me, shaking her head back and forth.

I pushed my emotions aside and focused on the task at hand. We had work to do, and there wasn't much time. "We only have fifteen minutes. That's not long, but it'll be enough. We need to take you home."

"What?" she asked.

"The Fae told us to bring you back to the village," a new voice, Jaria, added.

"Hello?" Evie said, turning toward the speaker.

"Jaria's with me. She's invisible—"

"You're apprenticed to the Mother," Evie continued, her tone warm with awe. She seemed pleased.

I tugged at her hand. "We need to go."

"You're sixteen?" She looked at the crystal at my neck. "How long ago did the Fae give you the pendant?"

"Summer Solstice," I said. "I started high school in August."

"Did they tell you why you can do this?" she asked.

Interesting question. I recalled Pa's argument

with Mother Gazina last fall. They had called this ability my birthright. Maybe my ma would understand what they meant. "No. Do you know why?"

She didn't answer but lifted a thumb to stroke my cheek. "I can't believe you're here..." At her touch, I flinched reflexively, and she pulled back. "It's good to see you."

"There isn't much time."

"How did you find me?" she asked. Despite my increasing sense of urgency, Evie would not be rushed.

"The Fae led me here." Jaria repeated what she'd told me the day before, concluding, "I made Alice persuasive so we could get past the gates."

"Wow." Evie seemed impressed by Jaria's tracking skills. "That's more than I could've done."

"You can do magic too?" I asked.

She shrugged. "I learned when I was an apprentice to the Mother."

If I was trained like a traditional apprentice, one allowed to meet with the Fae, I would know that. The thought jogged my memory—

"Your pendant, do you still have it?" I asked, and she nodded. "Let's get it. If you become invisible, then we can take you away using the car. It's simple. I'll persuade Dr. Oleski that—"

She shook her head and turned toward the place Jaria would be. "Did the Fae say why they need me?"

I gaped at her. We were rescuing her, and she was asking why.

"Not really," Jaria answered. "I asked, but they gave me a uselessly cryptic answer. Something about the Crux and the fading, but it also sounded like gibberish."

Jaria hadn't told me that, but if this concerned the Crux, our mission was important. The Crux hid the Bigfoot Village and kept Bigfoots beyond human awareness. *Fading* did not sound good.

Evie frowned but made no move toward her cabin. Something was wrong, something she wasn't saying.

Finally, I gathered my courage and asked, "What are you actually doing here?"

"Let me show you."

She led us to her cabin and invited us inside. It was a large room filled with an eclectic mix of furniture and belongings. Bed, kitchen, and a desk. A closet, a bathroom. It was a complete home.

My gaze lingered on the floor-to-ceiling bookshelves behind the desk. They were overflowing with books. A laptop charged at the desk's center, dwarfed by the stacks of books surrounding it.

The brightly covered books caught my eye. Their artwork and titles made them appear much more interesting than the volumes Jaria asked me to read.

"I've been busy," she said.

"Yes," I replied, still taking in the library she had collected. "But busy doing what?"

"I review books," she said. "I do it online. It's a great hobby, one where no one has to see my face. They just assume I'm human."

I stared at her.

She scratched her head. "I hoped to see you, but this wasn't what I expected."

"This—" I motioned toward the bookshelves. "This isn't what I expected either."

I scanned the bookshelf, discovering the wide range of books she'd collected. She had a bit of everything. Fantasy and memoirs, science fiction and romance, cookbooks and mysteries. There were books for children and others clearly intended for adults. Her interests seemed to have no limits.

The evidence of her new life was disconcerting, and I scratched at my itching stomach.

"Do you have your pendant?" I asked a second time. I didn't see it anywhere, but there were plenty of places to hide it.

She didn't respond.

I frowned, realizing that she wouldn't want to leave her books. As movies were essential to me, reading was necessary for her. And this was quite the collection.

"You're here under your own free will, aren't you?" I asked.

She looked down.

My anger grew. Her reactions told me the truth of my accusations. "You could have returned at any time." I ran my fingernails against inflamed skin.

"It's not so simple—my leg."

"The Fae need you now," Jaria added.

Evie sat on the bed, and it sighed under her weight. "I can't be who they need me to be."

I wished I felt pity, something—anything—other than rage. The skin of my belly grew hot. My vision tunneled.

"You abandoned me." I motioned to the cabin and pointed toward the bookshelves. "You abandoned me for this."

"I can't expect you to understand—"

"No, I can't." I began walking to the door.

"Please stay—I want to explain."

I pushed the door open.

Dr. Oleski stood outside, his hand poised like he was about to knock.

"Is everything okay?" he asked.

I forced my face into my sweetest smile, retreating into my guise as Alice Turner, expert of persuasion. "Everything is just perfect. Thanks so much for bringing me up here. Evie was just telling me about her excellent work as a reviewer."

"Well, glad you are getting along. Should we talk about what you saw last night?"

"No, we're good," I said. "I don't want to take up any more of Evie's time."

"It's nothing—" Evie cried.

"I'm going." I crossed the threshold and walked toward the stairs.

My heart raced, begging me to stop. I could still turn around. I could listen to her reasons. Maybe I could even convince her to return.

But I had no interest in persuading my unconcerned mother. The idea disgusted me. I tightened my smile, struggling to keep it bright.

"All right," Dr. Oleski turned to Evie. "Well, I hope you had a good visit."

"Alice is welcome back at any time!" Evie shouted after me.

"I have no reason to return." I hoped my words hurt her.

She rushed out of the cabin, chasing after me. "In case you change your mind—here." She forced something into my hand. "My contact information."

I shoved her business card in my pocket and walked away.

Chapter 9

"Alice, that was completely unnecessary," Jaria complained from the back seat of the Godparent Express as Flora drove down SEA's long driveway.

I adjusted my seat, pushing it back until I was practically lying in the second row, and closed my eyes.

"You're being ridiculous," she continued.

"Did you know she was here willingly? Be honest."

"No! The Fae helped me find her, I never thought—" She took a long breath. "I didn't expect this either. I'm bothered too, okay?"

"Well, we can't exactly drag her back to the village. If she doesn't want to come, we can't make her."

"You could have tried persuading her."

Persuade. I rubbed my belly through my shirt and *finally* reached under to scratch it with my fingernails. Relief, however brief, flooded my body. I dug my nails deeper.

"I've told you everything I know," Jaria said. "Stop being so sulky. Evie matters to me too. You're not the only one she left. She also abandoned me *and* your pa."

That stopped me for a moment, but the itching returned. I peeled my blouse up, inspecting my inflamed skin, finding that the sigil was peeling away.

Curious, I pinched the edge of the symbol, finding it was like tape stuck to my belly. I pulled it away, relieved to discover my skin no longer itched where the spell had been removed.

I sighed with the release and tore at the sigil, desperate to remove the entire thing. Anything to make the itching stop.

"Don't," Jaria complained. "I worked hard on that."

"I can't take this for another moment." I peeled the spell from my body. "If I had persuaded her, what would have happened when the spell was over?"

"We could have tried," Jaria huffed. "Now I'll have to explain everything to the Fae."

I wasn't in the mood to pity her. At least Jaria could meet the Fae; it was more than I could do. "If you're so nervous to talk to the Fae, bring me with you. I'll take the blame."

"No."

"Suit yourself." I destroyed the last of the sigil and pulled my blouse back over my liberated belly. It was still a little inflamed, but the worst had passed. The source of the itching was gone.

"Now that you've broken my spell, can we get back to business?" Jaria asked as we reached the fenced gate. "Even without the persuasion spell, Evie can still help us return to SEA. She wants to talk to you. Just say the word and we'll turn around."

I had no intention of returning and refused to reply. The gate rolled aside, and Flora drove back onto the highway.

If I never saw my ma again, our last interaction would be of me storming out of her lame rooftop home. It wasn't what I'd hoped for, but all my hopes were already dashed.

Neither Jaria nor I talked as we passed the university. Our silence remained unbroken when we reached the outskirts of Aldertown. And the more distance we traveled, the more final my decision became.

Maybe I'd see her again, maybe I wouldn't. Either way, I had to move on. I'd already grieved her death once. This should be nothing to me.

The sun set as we drove, casting the sky with hues of purple and pink. I watched the scenic view unfold, finding it completely uninspiring.

As we drove, I replayed the scene with Evie over and over until I couldn't remember what I had actually said. The truth muddled as new insults, ones I wished I'd said, began flooding my imagination.

Only once we approached the house did I dare to speak. During the drive, I had started planning, but there was information I needed from Jaria.

"When will you speak with the Fae?" I asked.

Jaria's reply was rigid. "Thursday night has the right lunar associations. I'll update you on Friday morning."

"You better tell me everything."

"I will."

But I didn't quite believe her. I couldn't afford to. She'd kept secrets from me before, and I expected her to do it again. Besides, my mind was made up, and my plan solidified.

It was time to finally see the Fae for myself.

Chapter 10

"I'll be in town today," I told Stepma and Bryson over breakfast Thursday morning. The news wouldn't surprise them, not after I'd spent all day Tuesday and Wednesday in my human home.

"More studying?" Stepma asked.

"Yes." A half-truth. I wasn't reading the books Jaria had given me—I couldn't even look at them without recalling Evie. Instead, I'd cruised from my bed to the couch, alternating between naps and the TV. All our frozen pizzas were baked, and all the ice cream was eaten.

It should have felt luxurious, but nothing soothed my irritation. No matter what I tried, I couldn't get comfortable. The movies had stopped being entertaining, and I had long grown tired of pizza and ice cream.

"I have big plans with Payton, so it might be a late night." A partial lie. I planned to see a movie with Payton, *and* I expected it to be a late night—but my evening plans involved following Jaria to the Fae.

"But I wanted to play," Bryson said. "Come with us to the community house." On a rainy day like today, the children would gather in the community house. It was the largest indoor space in the village and acted as both school room and playhouse.

"The greenhouses need extra help," Stepma offered. "Many of the seedlings are ready to be transplanted."

The community house had been fun once. Performing chores had once been my responsibility. "Payton is expecting me," I insisted.

"You said you'd play," Bryson complained.

It was true. I'd agreed to that once, back when past-me believed future-me would feel differently about this.

Bryson knew he was failing to convince me. He laid his forehead on the table and sprawled his hands over its surface. "Why are you always busy?"

"Sometime, when you're an adult, you'll understand," Stepma said.

Bryson squirmed back up, knocking over his glass of water in the process. He probably did it on purpose. Water pooled on the table.

"Grab a towel and clean that up," Stepma ordered.

Bryson huffed, but obeyed, tidying with as much drama as possible. I sank deeper into my chair, knowing my actions were just as bad—if not worse—I was just better at hiding it.

"Now, go upstairs and brush your fur," Stepma continued. "Be sure to clean the tufts behind your ears!"

He climbed into the loft, striking each rung of the ladder with a stomp. Stepma grabbed the broom and began sweeping the already-clean floor.

She was waiting for me to speak. Despite every concern racing in my mind, the silence, the need to tell someone I trust, drove me to speak. "I saw Evie on Monday."

She dropped the broom. It clattered on the floor.

"My birth ma. Evie. I saw her," I repeated.

Stepma closed her gaping mouth and put the broom away. "Is she okay? Is something wrong?"

"She's better than okay. In fact, she's doing great." I dipped my finger in my water glass and started smearing water on the table. Stepma glared at me, and I stopped. "Evie's stayed separate from the village on purpose."

She sat down beside me. "Tell me everything."

"I visited her on Monday," I whispered, ensuring my voice was too low for Bryson to hear. "She lives in a town a few hours away."

Stepma stared at me with... relief, maybe worry? Her expression grew increasingly inscrutable the longer she considered.

"It's a nice home, and she has lots of books."

Stepma laughed. "Does she? That sounds like Evie."

"The Fae asked us to bring her back. I thought she was a captive... But she's happy. Without me." My voice cracked. "I stormed out when I realized she'd stayed by choice."

Of anybody, why was I telling Stepma this? If I had to talk, Pa may have been the better choice.

"It might be possible for me to visit her again," I continued. "I could reach out to her—call her, email her—and I want her to answer my questions... Why did she leave?" And why wasn't I enough?

Stepma rested her hand over mine. "There's something your Pa and I need to tell you—"

Bryson clattered down the ladder. "I'm done! Can we go now?"

Stepma yanked her hand away from mine and wiped her cheek. Had she cried? "Let's go."

We stood, and she wrapped me in a hug.

"I'm ready!" Bryson called from the front door.

She released me and approached him. "Tell me three things you're excited for today."

He answered, babbling something I didn't listen to. Instead, I began shaking out my fur, hoping to steady myself.

Finally, Stepma turned back to me. "Go into town and see your friend. When you have the chance, you should tell Pa about this. He'd like to hear this from you."

I nodded, wondering what she would have said if Bryson hadn't interrupted. But then she and Bryson were gone, leaving me alone in the family cabin.

Chapter 11

I rang the doorbell of Payton's house while the Godparent Express idled in the driveway. Flora watched me, her human-mimicry spell making her stay until Payton opened the door. Because, *apparently*, that's what motherly figures were expected to do.

"Hey, Alice," Payton said as she opened the door. "Come on in."

The car backed away.

"Are you okay?" she asked.

I sighed, rubbing my forehead and stepping into the house. "It's complicated."

We entered the living room, and Payton scrambled to sit on the floor. She grabbed a bowl of popcorn she had ready.

I plopped onto the couch. "But how are you?"

"I'm pretty sure my life is less exciting than yours." She offered me the popcorn, but I turned her down. "I'm so tired. These morning shifts are worse than I expected. I go to bed early but can't fall asleep. Now I'm tired all the time."

"That's... hard." And I'd been so lazy.

"But in my haze of sleepy-sleeplessness, I had an idea."

"What are you thinking?"

"I've been thinking about *Goblins from Outer Space* and all the other movies we want to watch... What if we started a blog?"

"A blog?" I knew what a blog was but didn't understand why we'd write one.

"It'll be a place where we talk about movies. Maybe we could even meet others who like the same stuff as us!"

I tried to imagine what writing a blog would be like. Maybe it could be fun. Maybe it was even a way to convince Jaria that I needed to watch more movies—except...

My stomach twisted. "So, we'd be reviewing movies?"

"Yeah." She shook her head and scratched her neck. "I thought it was a good idea, but if you're not interested—"

"No, it's a great idea!" I insisted. "It's just..."

Her tone shifted, growing serious. "What happened?"

I rolled my shoulders and wiggled my butt deeper into the couch.

Payton said, "Well, whatever it is, I'm here. My last morning shift is tomorrow, and then I'm free all weekend."

She was far too generous. I hugged a decorative pillow to my stomach, and that reminded me of the itchy sigil. I shoved the pillow aside and looked to the ceiling. "Maybe we should go to Aldertown," I mumbled.

"Aldertown?"

I straightened in my seat and gave her my full attention. "I visited Aldertown on Monday with Jaria." Suddenly paranoid, I scanned the living room. "Your mom's at work, right?"

Payton nodded. "We're home alone."

I told her everything that had happened. From Jaria's itchy spellwork to Evie's beautiful garden—

Payton interrupted, "Is that why you want to visit Aldertown? I can help! Let's break your ma out of SEA!"

I shook my head. "There's a problem. She doesn't want to leave."

"What?"

"She isn't SEA's captive—she's their guest!" Saying it stirred my anger. "You should have seen her desk—covered with books—she's so comfortable with her life. She's practically human. Why would she want to return to the village? We don't even have running water, and there's definitely no internet. No books, no movies, and no blogs."

Payton pursed her lips as she considered her response.

"I guess," I continued, "she's nothing like I expected."

Payton handed me the popcorn, shaking the bowl until I accepted. I picked at a kernel, then two.

"Do you want to return to Aldertown?" she asked.

"Apparently? I don't know. What good will that do? I left for a reason. She chose to stay there, and I won't force her to return."

"But I guess..." Payton swallowed. "Maybe she had a reason. Did you ask her why?"

"No," I snapped. Payton frowned, and I relented. "I left before she could explain." *I left to keep her from explaining.*

"What if something kept her from returning?"

I considered her weakened leg, knowing it'd been healthy in my childhood. "It's possible that there are things I don't know."

We each grabbed a handful of popcorn.

Payton had a point, one that had been bothering me, even when I tried to ignore it.

"Either way, I'm tired of misinformation," I concluded. "And I've made a different plan."

"You're changing the subject."

"We can discuss going to Aldertown later, but Jaria is meeting with the Fae tonight. And I'm done with this intermediary nonsense and plan to track her. I want to eavesdrop on the Fae."

Payton furrowed her brow. "Are you sure that's a good idea? Aren't the Fae supposed to be crafty?"

I shrugged. Most of my knowledge came from Bigfoot legends. Despite their benign efforts to hide us from humans, the Fae were supposed to be tricksters.

"And how are you going to follow someone who can turn invisible?" Payton asked.

"Ah!" I smiled. "I've got an idea for that." I explained it to her, concluding, "So we need to go by the department store before the movie."

Payton looked at the clock. "We still have a few hours before *Goblins from Outer Space*. Want to cook lunch together? We can do an easy meal. Pasta, veggies, and red sauce?"

I considered saying no but then recalled all the frozen pizzas I had eaten. "That sounds nice. Besides, there needs to be something I can cook other than pizza."

While Payton wasn't as skilled at cooking as her mom, Tami had taught Payton everything she knew.

The effort kept my hands busy. Cutting vegetables as Payton instructed took all my focus. The work helped the time to pass as I nervously anticipated my chance to meet the Fae.

Jaria would warn me against seeing the Fae, reminding me that she was their intermediary and they didn't want to see me. But I was done caring about roles and expectations. After all, I worked for the Fae too.

The Fae were powerful—strong enough to create the Crux—but I wasn't afraid. Or maybe I was too angry to let fear stop me.

We rushed through the last of the dishes (Tami insisted that cleaning dishes was an essential part of cooking) and dashed from the kitchen to the department store. I purchased the special supply I needed to track Jaria, and we ran to the theater.

Goblins from Outer Space was everything we hoped it would be. The costumes were dramatic, and the acting over-the-top.

My favorite part was when the heroine learned to telepathically communicate with the strange green goblins. She realized that they only wanted peace and had never attacked Earth.

But then, a human—the general—had attacked Earth in a bid for power. During a nail-biting climax, the heroine and her new goblin friend stopped the general from launching a powerful missile. That scene was absolutely perfect.

The story ended with a festive banquet celebrating a peace treaty between humans and goblins. It should have been a happily ever after—but their feast was rudely interrupted by angry red aliens. They proclaimed their interest in taking over Earth and—

To be continued in Aliens from Another Galaxy, scrolled across the screen as the credit song played.

"Dang," Payton said.

My mouth was full with a final fistful of popcorn, but I mumbled my agreement.

"Do you want to see it again?" she asked. "How about tomorrow night? I'm not working, and I can't wait to watch the scene with the talking cow a second time."

I laughed. That had been a good scene, but tomorrow would be... Friday night. And I had a date with Mark. With everything else going on, I had forgotten to tell her!

"I've got plans tomorrow." With hushed whispers, I told her about Mark's note.

"Why didn't you tell me earlier?"

"I'm telling you now. I was going to explain on Friday after school, but Jaria—"

"You're going to have a human boyfriend!" She sang the words much louder than necessary.

"Shh!" I looked around. The credits were still rolling, and the theater was emptying. No one was listening to us. "Of course my boyfriend would be human... W-why wouldn't he be?"

"Of course." Payton chuckled, stood up, and stretched.

Once we left the theater, Payton darted to the nearest restroom as I lingered behind in the hallway.

Then I saw him. Mark.

My face burned with a blush, and I considered following Payton into the bathroom. But as I glanced at him again... he waved at me.

My lips twisted into a smile as I waved back. I recognized most of the boys surrounding him from school, presumably his friends. Should I talk to him or run away?

He walked toward me, and I froze in place.

"Hey," he began.

"Umm, hi." This was awful. I wished my heart would stop thumping. Surely he could hear it.

He looked at me with his excruciatingly blue eyes like he was peering into me. They always made me feel vulnerable, a sensation that normally scared me, but with Mark, I always felt brave enough to be myself. He made it okay to be different.

He scratched his nose. "So, how's the movie?"

"Goblins?" I asked, and he nodded. "Oh, it was great. What did you think?"

"We're here for the next showing." He nodded toward his friends. They were trying to toss popcorn into each other's mouths.

"Umm..." I was not used to seeing him outside of school. "How's your spring break going?"

"Good. Lots of time with my friends—the ones throwing popcorn all over the floor. Maybe I should stop associating with them. How about your week?"

I laughed at his joke. "Honestly, it's been a little strange... There's been some family drama."

"Yikes."

"Yeah, it's... messy."

Payton stepped from the bathroom and began watching us from across the hall.

"Listen, I've got to go—" I motioned toward Payton. "But enjoy the movie."

"About Friday—"

"Mark, let's go." A girl pulled at his arm. A pretty girl. "I've got the popcorn, so let's find our seats before all the good ones are taken. I'm so excited about this movie!"

He smiled at her. He was cute when he smiled.

But it wasn't cute that he smiled at her.

My stomach plummeted. Why was he seeing *Goblins from Outer Space* with a girl? He had made fun of me for wanting to see this movie. Now he was seeing it with this random girl?

"Uh, nice to see you." I darted for the bathroom, and Payton followed.

"Alice—" he began.

But I was already gone, running toward the sink. My hands clutched the counter, and I worked to breathe.

"You're taller than him," Payton said, standing calmly beside me. "I have history class with him, but I'd never seen you two standing side by side and—"

"Do you know that girl?" I asked.

"I don't. But I didn't think... He seems into you."

I grumbled, unable to speak.

"There has to be an explanation," Payton continued. "Ask him about it tomorrow night." She waited for my reply. "You'll still go, won't you?"

I shrugged, too busy holding down my lunch to answer. My mind whirled, imagining reason after reason for why he could be deceiving me. It seemed like everyone was hiding something.

And I was no exception.

Chapter 12

I returned to the Bigfoot Village late in the afternoon. After a quick stop by the house to give Jaria her present, I headed for the hunting pavilion. I needed to talk to Pa.

The pavilion stood at the outskirts of the farmland, tucked against the Bigfoot Forest's edge. It was far enough from the village that I'd rarely approached it. After all, I was female, and hunting was a masculine trade.

A few storage sheds surrounded the central hunting pavilion. It had a large circular roof held in place by pillars. Several animal hides hung from the posts, creating makeshift walls that shielded its inhabitants from the snow and rain. They did nothing to protect against the cold. After all, a worthy hunter had no reason to fear the cold.

As I approached, I heard the grinding of metal against stone, the sound of weapons being sharpened. Shouts filled the air as the males trained. Some practiced in the neighboring archery range, others threw spears in a nearby clearing, but most were under the pavilion. That was where they sparred.

I felt the heat of their many gazes, and I struggled to stand tall. Females were free to approach the pavilion—but it rarely happened. Once, someone would have already asked me to explain my presence. Now that I was an apprentice to the Mother, no one questioned me.

Fortunately, I didn't need to wander long. Pa sat in front of a shed, restringing a series of bows.

His forehead creased as I neared, but I didn't balk. Faking confidence worsened my nausea, but I wanted to look like I belonged. At least for a few minutes.

"Alice." Pa set a bow aside, folded his arms over his chest, and peered at me.

I was afraid that I'd crossed a line by coming here. Maybe I should have met with him at home, somewhere we could have talked in private. But I wanted answers—now.

"I have something to tell you," I began.

He waited for me to continue.

"It's about my ma. Evie."

He raised an eyebrow.

"She's alive."

His gaze intensified. The others stared at us. While no one stood close enough to overhear, Pa's tension showed in his stiff posture.

"It's true, she's alive. I saw her."

"Really?" His eyes glistened, the first hint of warmth.

"Really. I visited her on Monday."

"Is she safe?"

"Yes. She's living in a beautiful garden and has lots of books."

His demeanor relaxed. He laughed, possibly a little forced and certainly louder than necessary. With his signal, the bustle of training resumed around us.

"After all these years, I still hoped." He pointed to a nearby stool. "Why don't you tell me everything?"

I pulled the stool closer to him, grateful Pa had publicly accepted my presence, and yet, his attitude toward this...

He smiled. "Did you know Evie named you after a character in a book? *Alice's Wanderings in Adventureland* or something."

"Alice's Adventures in Wonderland," I corrected. My throat grew dry as I struggled to interpret his reactions. His smile kept growing bigger, more genuine—and yes, news of Evie should make him happy—but he showed none of the conflict I expected. What did this mean for Stepma, my family?

"She doesn't want to return," I said, frustration heating my words.

"Ah." He nodded but didn't appear hurt by the revelation.

"She stayed away from us," I continued.

But still, nothing. Just his vague, humored smile. I bit my lip, cutting my urge to lash out.

He must have seen it on my face, for his grin faded, and his mouth shaped words he never started. Eventually, he delivered his disappointing reply, "Alice, everything is more complicated than you know."

"Complicated? Everything is complicated!" I shook my head, trying to work the frustration from my body. "I'm sick of it!" I complained. "Stepma acted the same way—"

"You told Sarene?" he asked.

"I told her before you," I snapped. "It's like she's my real ma and Evie is—Evie is—" I gasped, finding it impossible to finish the sentence.

"Evie is who she is," he concluded. "Just like you."

"What's that supposed to mean?"

He huffed. "Give me a minute to think."

I hmphed in reply, but otherwise, grew quiet.

My gaze wandered. I considered the strong hunters surrounding me, evaluating their training grounds and weapons. I turned toward the fighting box centered under the pavilion.

I'd watched fights before—competitions were often part of our festivals—but this was different. Less pomp, more raw. A few of the hunters glanced my way, their expressions tinged by the tension of my presence.

Two hunters prepared for a bout. They clapped hands, nodded, and dropped into their stances. A referee turned an hourglass and shouted for the match to begin.

I watched, transfixed, as they began circling each other, contemplating their best angle to attack. Victory went to whoever pushed their opponent outside the chalk lined fighting box.

"Evie was never truly happy among our people," Pa finally said. "Even when we were children."

"You two grew up together. You were neighbors, right?" I watched as one of the males kicked and then punched his foe out of the ring. They centered and started round two.

"Evie and I grew up together, always playing together like you and Jaria did. Then Mother Gazina asked Evie to become an apprentice. Evie came home with that crystal and then—disappeared. She vanished for weeks. Do you remember how strange it was when Jaria vanished? It was a little like that."

I nodded. Jaria had disappeared without a trace. The adults told me not to worry, offering vague promises that she'd return, but nobody explained why. The rites of the Mother were frustratingly mysterious, practically taboo.

"A few weeks later, Evie found me while I was hunting alone," Pa continued. "She needed someone to talk to, a friend, and explained everything. She told me that the pendant gave her invisibility, that she was living with the Fae to learn their magic, and that she would be visiting the humans.

"It was difficult for me to understand, but I knew she needed my help. And the least I could do was listen. We began meeting every week while she was in training. And as the years passed, I watched as she became infatuated with humans."

I considered how complete the Fae's collective knowledge was and wondered how much of it had been Evie's work.

"When her years with the Fae ended, she began living in the Mother's house. And while she helped Mother Gazina, she continued studying humans. She was transfixed, but through it all, our friendship remained—"

"And then she became pregnant," I interrupted, saving him from explaining. Nobody had told me this, but I'd suspected it for some time. The Mother's mate was the village, not a male. After all, this was the obstacle that had ended my courtship with Daylen last fall.

"And then she became pregnant with you," Pa agreed. "And she gave up the possibility of becoming the Mother."

His explanation did nothing to quench my frustration. "That doesn't help me understand. I've told you and Stepma that Evie's alive and both of you act like... like it doesn't matter that she's chosen to stay away."

He smacked his lips. "There is more to the story." He pulled at the bow string and looked around. "But

I won't say more. Not here. Sarene and I will tell you together."

"Promise?" I asked.

Yet he hesitated.

"Promise?" I insisted.

"Promise," he agreed. "Alice, I've only tried to shield you—"

"Well, stop. I'm not a child. Not anymore."

"No, you're not." He sighed. "You've grown up much faster than I expected."

I laughed a little at that, and he studied me quizzically. "You're right. A lot has changed since Summer Solstice."

"It has been a strange year for you."

I nodded and looked back at the fighting ring. The male who had won the first round had lost the second but dominated the third. Two out of three. He secured his victory for the match.

Two new contestants stepped forward, and my jaw clenched as I recognized them. Heron and Daylen would spar each other next.

I hated to admit it, but Daylen looked good. The winter had strengthened him, and the sight of him made my breath catch.

"Nila ended their suitorship," Pa told me as if it wasn't important.

Considering the way I flushed at the news, it mattered.

I shifted forward in my seat, and Pa chuckled. I hit his arm in return, unsure of what he was insinuating. Rekindling a relationship with Daylen would not be simple. There was my apprenticeship to consider, and the fact that I'd already rejected him.

Daylen looked up to meet my gaze, and my body tensed under his attention. He waved and grinned, oh-so-casually showing how pleased he was by my presence. The referee turned the hourglass and signaled for their match to begin.

Honestly, I expected Daylen to lose. He himself had told me that Heron usually won their competitions. It was his greatest insecurity.

Yet he quickly dominated the round. Daylen darted the moment the referee signaled to begin. He forced Heron across the line with a dynamic series of punches and kicks.

I clapped, and Daylen grinned. I wished he'd look at me again... But no such luck. The second round was starting, and he set his sights on Heron.

I tapped my feet as they began circling each other.

Heron wasn't so easy to surprise the second time, and he blocked Daylen's initial attack. They darted back and forth until the hourglass was nearly empty. In the final seconds, Heron found the upper hand, forcing Daylen from the ring.

They stepped aside, pausing before beginning the third round. Whoever won this would win the match.

"You've got it, Daylen!" I shouted.

I clapped a hand over my mouth. The words had been impulsive. I'd yelled like I would during a volleyball match. But others shouted too, and nobody seemed to care that I'd joined their cheers. Maybe I hadn't been heard—

But Daylen looked at me and grinned. We made eye contact, and my flush returned. Then he shifted his weight, bouncing in preparation for the last round.

The referee signaled, and they began again.

Daylen moved first, attempting to push Heron aside. But Heron dodged, pushing his mass into Daylen's side. The power of his momentum forced

Daylen backwards. He stumbled but regained control a hand's width from the chalk-lined edge.

Heron circled him, searching for an opportunity to deliver the final blow.

Daylen shifted his weight leftward, preparing an attack. But, as Heron moved to block, Daylen feinted. He pushed Heron off balance and then forced him beyond the fighting box.

The referee signaled. Daylen had won!

I leaped to my feet, clapping as loudly as the others. Daylen grinned at me, his smile piercing my heart.

A familiar regret resurfaced. I could have been his mate; we could have shared a future together. A future that—apparently—I still wanted.

But.

But what if I was just like Evie? What if we became mates and I chose humanity over him a second time?

Pa grunted.

I looked at the ground.

"You could always step away from your apprenticeship," Pa said. "You could still rejoin our community."

"I don't know if I can."

"I would help you speak with the Elders. Give it some thought, okay? You two shared something special."

"We did," I admitted. "And if I'm being honest, there's a part of me that..." I shook my head. "What if I leave him, like she left us?"

He grunted. "Alice, I only want what is best for you. I don't understand humans, not like you or Evie do, but I do care for you. You're spectacular and deserve the best."

His words caught me by surprise. Pa was not free

with his affections.

I looked up again and searched for Daylen. His friends clustered around him; they were laughing. He didn't approach me, and I didn't walk over to him.

"I'll see you later," I said, standing up. "I won't be home for dinner—actually, it might be another late night—but I hope we can finish this conversation soon."

"We will. And you'll think about..." He motioned to the group of young males, to Daylen.

"I will."

Chapter 13

While I wasn't exactly sure when Jaria would visit the Fay, I knew it would be after dark. Sunset approached, and I needed to choose my hiding place. I returned to the village with an extra bounce in my gait.

Pa agreed to tell me everything. And tonight, I would follow Jaria to the Fae. While I still had plenty of questions, I was taking steps toward clarity.

I stopped by the food stores at the edge of the village and darted inside. Nobody paid me any notice as I filled my satchel with nuts, dried fruit and jerky—the perfect snacks for a stakeout.

Next, I neared the Mother's house. Hopefully, Jaria was there as she typically ate dinner with Mother Gazina. I just had to find somewhere to hide—

"Alice!"

I turned to find Bryson looking at me.

"Where's Stepma?" I asked.

"Inside," he pointed toward the cookhouse. "She already has tonight's stew, but now she's stuck talking."

I laughed. Stepma liked to chat.

"I thought you had plans today." Bryson shifted on his feet.

"I do..." It bothered me to deceive Stepma, but lying to Bryson was worse. I waved my satchel. "But I needed some extra snacks."

"Will I see you tomorrow?"

"Of course." After tonight, I would have information from the Fae. Soon Pa and Stepma would tell me what they wanted to explain. Then, with everything resolved, I could give my brother the attention he deserved.

"If you say so." He rubbed his foot against the dirt.

The sun would set soon. "I need to go. Don't tell Stepma you saw me. I don't want her to worry."

"Okay."

"Thank you." I handed him a dried strawberry, his favorite.

A new smell lingered on the air... The exact scent I was waiting for.

"Tomorrow?" he asked.

"Uh..." The scent grew stronger. "Sorry, I've got to go."

I rushed away from him, tracking that sweet smell. It was the distinctive scent I had been expecting.

My plan had worked. Jaria was near.

Before the movie, I had purchased a bottle of perfume to give to Jaria. Since I could hear her while she was invisible, I figured I could smell her too. It seemed to have worked. And now her floral smell distinguished her from everything else in the village.

I hid behind a tree as Jaria and Mother Gazina entered the Mother's house. A few minutes later, Jaria reemerged, and the scent intensified. She began walking away, and I darted, shifting from the shadows of one tree to another.

She only visited the cookhouse. She said

something to Bryson before stepping inside and shortly returned with a pot of stew and loaf of bread. I followed her as she brought her dinner back to the Mother's house.

Once the door was closed, I clambered up the nearest tree and found a comfortable branch. Then the waiting began.

The stakeout proved to be much more boring than expected. This was not like the movies. I ate my little dinner of snacks, growing impatient with every bite.

Dusk descended, and nothing happened. The full moon rose, and nothing changed. I tapped my finger against the tree. A gust of wind ran through my fur, and I shivered.

She would come out soon. She had to. But no. Not yet.

"Come on, Jaria," I whispered, fighting another shiver.

I waited in the dark and the cold. My stomach grumbled, asking for a proper dinner. I shifted to a different branch, finding a place with better shelter from the gusty winds.

The moon drifted in and out of sight from behind the clouds, illuminating the night with its ghostly glow. Stars sparkled through the haze, diminished by the brighter moon.

Time had long begun to blur when finally— *finally*—the door opened again. Nobody appeared to have opened it, but I took a deep breath and smelled the truth.

Jaria stood there.

Carefully, I dropped from the tree, ensuring my feet struck the ground without a noise. While I couldn't see where she walked, I could track her.

At least, that was the plan. Unfortunately, the gusting winds made the work extra difficult, and the effort took all my focus.

I followed her northward, past the edge of the village, beyond the farmland, and deep into the surrounding forest. We kept walking, approaching the boundary.

We neared Northridge and climbed the last of the switchbacks to reach the small clearing beneath the highest peak. It was an area I had rarely visited since it was so far from the village, but now that I understood signs of the Fae, it was clear that this place was magical.

At the center of the clearing, five tree stumps formed a circle. The formation was too perfect to be natural. I lingered behind a shrub, unsure if I wanted to step into the open.

Jaria appeared in the clearing. She lifted her pendant from her neck and wrapped the cord around her wrist. The clouds had cleared, and thanks to the full moon, it was easy to see her. She walked to the space between the tree stumps.

"Jaria's here?"

I spun around. Bryson. How long had he been following me? "What are you doing?" I whispered.

"You looked like you were playing a game. I thought if I followed you, I could play too," Bryson explained.

I rubbed my palm against my forehead. "How have you been—" I sighed. It didn't matter. He was here.

How had I failed to notice him tracking me? But the gusting wind had made it so difficult to follow Jaria… And I never suspected someone would follow me.

I looked back at Jaria. She was standing in the center of the circled stumps.

Bryson tugged at my hand. "Are you playing hide and seek with Jaria? You're cheating."

I turned to him and ripped my hand from his grip. And when I looked for Jaria again... She was gone.

I shifted and squinted, trying to get a better look. Maybe she had hidden somewhere out of sight. But nothing helped. Even her scent dissipated.

"She's vanished," Bryson said with awe.

"This isn't normal hide-and-seek." I began thinking fast. "This game has a special set of rules."

"Can I play? Tell me the rules."

"Promise me you'll do exactly as I say."

"I will!"

I swallowed, guilt tightening my stomach. I considered leaving and walking him home, but I needed to see the Fae and had already come so close.

"All right." I thumped his nose with my finger. "Now you're part of the game. Do you smell that sweet scent?"

It had become barely detectable, but he nodded.

"That's Jaria. She's hiding now. You can help me find out where she went."

I ran to the center of the stumps, encouraging him to follow me. My deception bothered me, but there was nothing dangerous here. And even if we met the Fae, they couldn't be that bad—they were the protectors of our village. They wouldn't hurt Bryson.

We circled the stumps.

"I don't see her." Bryson fell to his knees and began crawling on the grass.

I laughed at him. "Why are you doing that? What would she do, disappear into the ground?"

Except, well, this was the Fae. Maybe she had

gone downward.

"The smell is strongest in the center." Bryson crawled that way.

He was right, the scent was stronger near the ground. Feeling ridiculous, I began to crawl.

Bryson reached the center first. He grabbed at the earth, searching in a manner that hadn't even occurred to me.

"I found something!" he called.

"Where?"

He pointed.

"That's a rabbit hole," I said. "Jaria wouldn't—"

—*ah-choo*—

I sneezed. My nose tingled in a now-familiar way. Magic.

Grasping, I dug my hand into the hole. My skin grew itchy. Making a guess to how the spell might work, I brought my other palm to the opening and pressed it open.

The hole widened. I kept pulling, forcing it to become big enough for us to fit. It opened to a cave-like tunnel below, and the scent of flowers grew strong again.

How far had Jaria gone? Hopefully, I could still catch up.

I sneezed again and, before I lost my nerve, jumped into the tunnel. The cave's ceiling was barely taller than my head. Returning to the surface would be a little tricky—

Bryson dropped into the cave beside me.

I prepared to chastise him, to tell him the game was over and he won, but he ran, his path illuminated by glowing crystals. He chased after the scent.

Maybe coming here was a mistake, but Bryson was already gone. I chased after him.

Chapter 14

I reached Bryson as the tunnel opened into a larger chamber. He stood at the threshold, awestruck by the room beyond. I grabbed his shoulder but failed to speak. This cavern was beautiful.

A waterfall pounded, water pouring from a higher source into a crystalline pond that filled this side of the cavern. The cave appeared to be large, but it looked impossible to reach the other side without swimming.

More crystals illuminated the chamber, but there was a stronger light source—the moon. The roof of the chamber had a small opening, and through it, moonlight cast eerie shadows.

Something shifted. My eyes tracked it, finding Jaria. She darted around the waterfall, following a path that ran behind it.

"Should we chase after her?" Bryson asked.

The light seemed to grow brighter. I attempted to answer Bryson's question. "She's hiding. Now we wait."

The pond glistened, reflecting the moonlight and scattering it across the cavern. Then moonrays shifted, turning in unnatural ways. Suddenly, beings emerged from the refracted light.

"You and Jaria play strange games," Bryson

whispered.

"Shh." While I had never seen them before, the figures materializing around us were undeniably Fae.

They rose from the moonrays. At first, they seemed transparent, but as the seconds passed, their bodies grew solid. It was like they were passing from one realm into another.

The Fae appeared in many different forms. Most were human height, but some were so small they could have stood on my palm. Others stood tall like giants. Some had wings, and others flew by other means. They all had pointed ears, and each was breathtakingly beautiful.

A frolic of smaller winged Fae flitted our direction, and glitter trailed behind them. Faerydust. It glistened in a rainbow of colors as it drifted our way.

There were so many of them. They began filling the cavern.

Two Fae leapt across the pond, dancing to music I didn't hear. As they spun, Faerydust whirled out, swirling toward us.

I considered running, but found I couldn't look away.

Fae children started chasing each other up and down our shore. They flitted upward and fell back down.

Wouldn't it be fun to fly?

Bryson giggled and stood. He took a step toward them—

I yanked his shoulder, pulling him away. "Don't let them see us." I brushed Faerydust from his fur, fighting back a sneeze.

"But they're having so much fun!" He wiggled from me, forcing more of the dust into the air.

I coughed and sneezed. Bryson got away.

He ran, leaping into the chamber, giggling like the Fae children who now surrounded him. They invited him into their game. Together, they laughed and pranced and jumped.

"Bryson!" I yelled. "Come back!"

One of the Fae must have heard me, for she walked my way, smiling as if we shared a secret. She was wingless and had impossibly violet eyes that matched her hair.

Transfixed, I watched as she combed Faerydust from her hair, collecting it in her palm. She blew me a kiss, scattering the glittery powder across my face. Maybe it made my nose itch, but...

Want to dance?

I couldn't resist a moment longer.

Together, arm in arm with the violet-haired Fae, we skipped into the chamber. My body felt itchy, but the discomfort was so small compared to my delight.

I laughed. The sound resonated in my chest, and my entire body shook with glee. I finally, finally felt joy. Why had I been in such a mood?

Bryson turned toward me and leapt a few feet in the air, the Fae children helping him jump. I grabbed him under the armpits and lifted him upward, like I had done when he was smaller, only now with magical assistance. I spun him around, and he squealed. He giggled uncontrollably as I lowered him back to the ground.

We spun and danced, following the rhythm within us. Again and again... I could dance until my feet were worn raw.

"Alice!"

Someone was shouting. I heard them and forgot. The Faerydust continued to fall, and by now my entire body glittered.

"Alice!"

Everything itched, but even as my skin burned, Bryson and I danced harder, faster.

Fae grabbed my elbows, while others held my feet. More lifted Bryson. Working together, they hoisted us upward and off the ground.

"Higher, higher!" Bryson gasped between laughs.

I loved his giggles. Even if they were becoming manic.

More Fae joined us, lifting us higher. The ground was looking far away. Maybe I should be scared. The less fun me would have been scared—

Water slapped my legs. The Fae dropped me, and I fell. Another slap of water struck me, and I watched the glitter drip from my body.

Cold, confusing reality returned to me. But Bryson—

Bryson was laughing at me like this was terribly funny. The Fae still held him... carrying him across the pond...

I ran to the water's edge.

"Don't touch it!" Jaria shouted after me. "That water is worse than the Faerydust."

That stopped me. Slowly, I turned to look at her. She was holding a bucket of water. "But Bryson!"

"Why is he even here? I know you're foolish enough to follow me. But why him? He's a child!"

"Is he going to be all right?"

She didn't answer me. "Let's go to the waterfall. It'll keep the Faerydust away."

"I can't leave Bryson!"

"He'll be okay."

I longed to question her, but this wasn't the time to fight.

I followed her behind the waterfall. There was a ledge that extended the entire distance, creating a pathway to the other side of the cavern. The thunderous sounds of the waterfall filled the air. I inhaled, finding the breath heavy with mist. The last of my whimsical mood vanished.

"You used the perfume, didn't you?" Jaria shouted, barely audible over the crashing water.

"Yes!" I yelled back. "How am I going to get Bryson back?"

"He's not the first child to wander into a Fae cave. Not everyone's allergic to magic like you."

"I'm not—" I stopped scratching my arm. Now that she mentioned it... the itching intensified.

"Put your arm in the waterfall," she instructed.

"You said don't touch the water!"

"The waterfall is different than the pool," she said, making it sound obvious. "Alice! This is why you shouldn't be here. It's dangerous. Thankfully they like children..."

I thrust my arm into the water, relieved that the itching stopped. "I never meant to bring Bryson. He followed me."

She considered for a long second. More questions and complaints circulated through my mind, but I held my tongue.

Jaria shifted. "I know I haven't exactly been free with information. Not since the Fae chose me."

There was something in her expression that caught me off guard, a vulnerability that hadn't been there before.

While we had snipped at each other for months, we never talked about why. We never discussed the incident with Lexi. Nor did we discuss how Jaria had disappeared for two years without any explanation—

how, when she did return, she'd rejected my attempts at friendship.

Her time with the Fae had changed her. I'd tried to be a good friend and ask her about it, but she'd never given me a straight answer.

I looked around the ledge, finding practical items like a drinking glass and a bowl. There was a metal carving and a doll—one I recognized from our childhood. Had Jaria lived here?

I'd been too frustrated by her rejection to wonder if she didn't talk about the Fae because it was too painful.

"Ahem!" A cough. Then a surly voice. "Her Highness does not like to be kept waiting."

"Right." Jaria sucked in a breath, grabbed my wrist, and muttered, "If there was a moment for you to just trust me—for Bryson's sake—this is it." She pulled me to the other side of the cavern.

A Fae woman, glittering and practically swelling with magic, waited for us—but I had no eyes for her. Not when Bryson... Bryson still danced, still giggled. He did not understand what was happening. Maybe I could shout for him...

"Queen Avilana," Jaria said, pulling my hand as she dropped into a deep curtsy. I mimicked her as best I could, fighting my impulse to run to my brother. For Bryson's sake, I would do what Jaria asked.

We rose from our curtsy, and I studied Queen Avilana. She had the height of a child and bore oversized wings. The tip of her ears was sharper than most, and unlike every other Fae in the room, she had no color. Her hair, wings, and even her skin were silver.

Her gray eyes sliced through me. "Alice. We were

not expecting you, but I suppose it is time we've properly met. Although, I warn you, do not visit us uninvited ever again. Being in your presence is quite unpleasant." She smiled, baring all her teeth.

I was unpleasant? Did I smell?

"So," Avilana asked Jaria, "where is Evie?"

Jaria shifted her weight. "She... didn't want to come."

"But surely..." Avilana threw her hands into the air. "Oh, I should have expected Evie to be difficult. It is her way."

"I'm sure Alice and I can convince her," Jaria continued. "As I hope you'll understand, she was startled to see us. We just need more time."

Avilana sniffed. "It's not like we have a choice. Do this for us, Jaria. After all, now we have leverage."

Leverage? What did they have over Jaria?

But Jaria's gaze shifted, turning toward Bryson.

"No." I jumped aside, ready to run to him.

But I'd barely taken a few steps before two of Avilana's guards grabbed my shoulders. They were stronger than their lanky bodies suggested.

Avilana gave a shrill giggle. "I can't recommend that," she said.

"Fine." I stopped squirming, and the guards released me. I turned to Avilana, to Bryson, thinking quickly. "Take me, not Bryson." I fell to my knees before her. "It's my fault. I got angry with Evie. Don't make him stay."

She tutted. "Alice, I had no idea you were so funny."

I waited, hoping.

"Up, up," she commanded. "I'll do no such thing. Your presence is distasteful enough, not that you can help it, but you will never remain in our caves. Bryson will be much more fun than you'd ever be. Besides, Jaria could use your help bringing Evie back."

I met her gaze. "And if I convince Evie to return, you'll release Bryson?"

She nodded.

"Why do you even want her? She wanted to know."

Avilana lifted an eyebrow. "For consultation, of course. About the fading."

Consultation? The fading? "What does that—"

"It's a generous offer," Jaria interrupted. "Alice would be wise to accept."

But her offer wasn't good enough for me. "What if I promise—I'll swear on anything—what if I agree to bring Evie back? Then can Bryson return with us?"

"*You* cannot promise on anything of ours," the Fae said. "Besides, he's having such a wonderful time." As if on cue, his newest giggle filled the cavern. "It'd be a shame to end his playtime early. It's not like you've been giving him the company he wants."

Avilana's observation was uncomfortably accurate, and my frustration bubbled anew. She grinned, cat-like, as if she knew exactly how this would aggravate me.

Fortunately, Jaria asked, "You'll keep him in accordance with the Crux's Pact?"

Avilana's face darkened, shadows shifting to sharpen her prideful cheekbones. "A Queen of Fae would never break the Pact."

Jaria turned to me. "He'll be fine. There are rules."

I didn't know the rules, and nothing I'd seen was reassuring. Jaria's time with the Fae had clearly left scars.

"Your ma's been here—and Sarene," Jaria added.

"Stepma?" I asked. Why would she have been

here?

Avilana clapped her hands. "Is it decided then? If you promise to go quickly, I'll even let you say goodbye to him."

"Do it," Jaria instructed.

My throat choked. This wasn't acceptable. I refused to leave without Bryson. Since the day he'd been born, I'd promised the Fae I'd protect him. I couldn't...

I looked to Jaria. "Is this really your best advice?"

She nodded.

"Okay," I told Avilana. "I'll bring Evie back, and when I do, Bryson returns with me."

Chapter 15

My goodbye with Bryson hardly counted as one. He wouldn't focus and demanded that we dance. I obliged, spinning him a few times, mimicking joy I couldn't feel, grasping whatever I could from those few seconds.

Too soon, Jaria led me back to the safety of the waterfall.

"I'll be back soon," I whispered as we left.

My stomach tightened, twisting as I tried to digest everything that had just happened. Bryson was with the Fae, and I needed to face Evie. And the Fae—I shook my head—the Fae were confusing.

"Why don't they like me?" I whispered to Jaria as we trudged through the tunnel.

She didn't answer, and I didn't try asking again.

Still speechless, we reached the rabbit hole. Jaria muttered words too low to be heard, and the opening expanded, becoming big enough for us to pass through.

Jaria leaped with a quick, forceful bound that was too powerful to be natural. I shimmied up after her, struggling to pull my body over the edge—and I slipped back down.

I tried again and fell.

Jaria peered over the edge. She shook her head,

stamped her foot, and finally, howled. Her furry face blocked the moon.

I shuddered at the sound. My muscles tensed, everything tightening with the sound of her howl. And when she finished, Jaria glanced back at me like it hadn't happened. She sighed.

"Jump while holding your pendant," she explained.

"Oh," I sighed. Doing as instructed, I gained the same unnatural strength she had shown. I bounded to the surface, making it through, but missing my landing. I fell on my butt.

She spoke down to me, "Alice, I'll only say this once, so please listen. I don't hate you, and I'm really trying to help you. Sometimes I'm guarded, and I understand you want me to open up, but—Seriously, stop pretending I don't have your best interests at heart."

I didn't know how to reply. Jaria's fury wasn't fiery, and she didn't incite me to fight back. Her rage was like ice.

She continued, "I have my reasons for being who I am. Did you really believe the Fae were good or kind or straightforward to live with?" Her brow furrowed. "I learned to hide everything about myself."

"I wish I could have helped—"

"And now your selfishness brought Bryson to the Fae."

She was right. I'd made a mistake, and Bryson would pay for it. My breathing became sticky. "I can't believe myself." I huffed. "I messed up." Inhale. "I-I—"

I stood, swaying side to side. The consequences of my choices refused to settle. Instead, they burned in my stomach, my chest, my head...

"I'm so sorry." Gasp. "For everything."
I ran away.

No matter how fast I lifted my legs, I failed to outpace my self-hatred. I locked my gaze to the moonlit path. I ran and ran and ran...

Bryson's with the Fae. It's my fault.

My foot caught on a rock. I gasped, falling, tripping, tumbling... and sat back up. Nothing broken. My shin would probably bruise. I stood and ran again.

But it was impossible to escape my frustration.

Stepma and Pa won't trust me anymore.

My feet pounded against the dirt.

I'm a monster. A selfish monster.

My foot landed in shadow and slid out from under me. I fell again. This time, my knee exploded with pain.

I righted myself and tried to stand, but my knee didn't take my weight. Anguish pushed me back to the ground.

My nausea rose. My heart raced. I pressed my forehead into the earth and slammed my fist against the ground.

I began to cry. Big Bigfoot tears. Ugly Bigfoot howls.

Moments passed, and with time, the chaos quieted. Nothing felt better, but I could think.

I had made a gigantic mistake. But there was a way to correct it.

I needed to talk with Evie. For Bryson's sake, I would go forward.

Sitting in the dirt wasn't helpful. I crawled forward until I found a stick that could bear my weight. Using it to stand, I discovered my knee could take some weight.

I hobbled to the village. Onward.

Chapter 16

First things first, I needed to explain everything to my parents. I entered our family's cabin, both relieved and terrified to find both Pa and Stepma inside. They sat at the table with Mother Gazina and Jaria.

Clearly, they'd already been told everything.

I froze at the threshold but dared to hold Stepma's gaze, desperately trying to communicate my regret. I searched for her reactions. Reading Pa was easy; his anger and frustration were palpable. Stepma remained inscrutable.

Mother Gazina stood, and Jaria followed suit. As the Mother considered me, I withered under her attention.

"Jaria's already explained," Gazina said. "There's nothing more for us to do tonight." She led Jaria toward the door.

I didn't step aside. "Jaria." I reached for her. "I..." Words failed me. My plan had been to apologize. I wanted to say I was sorry for every expectation I had forced on to her, for every moment I'd refused to acknowledge who she'd become... but no words seemed adequate.

She stared at me, and I hoped she could see something of what was struggling within me.

Eventually, she straightened her back, showing the dignity that befit her position. "We'll leave for Aldertown at sunrise."

"Thank you," I managed in reply.

That was it. I stepped aside, and they left the cabin.

I settled into an empty chair and grabbed an unused cup. I poured the last of the water into it and discovered my hands were shaking. Stepma rested her fingers over my wrist, and I clenched the cup.

"Please don't hate me," I blurted out. "I can't stand myself, if that's any consolation."

"We don't hate you," she said, "but we are disappointed."

I nodded. Me too. "Is Bryson safe? Jaria said he would be, something about the Crux's Pact. Is she right? Either way, I'll see Evie tomorrow, I'll do anything—"

"He's safe." Stepma ran her fingers over my hand in an effort to calm me. "The Pact protects visiting Bigfoot from the worst of the Fae. They also delight in our children. He will be okay."

Pa grumbled.

"He may be a little... changed," Stepma admitted.

"No!" I tried to pull away, but Stepma held my wrist.

"I spent a few days in the cave as a child," she continued. This was news to me. "If anything, Bryson will develop a greater affinity for their magic."

I tried to imagine Stepma as a child, playing as Bryson was doing now. Giggling and spinning and dancing. She always had been unusually connected to the Crux...

Maybe he was safe, but Bryson would still be changed because of me. But wasn't he already asking strange questions because he was my brother? I squirmed. "What happens if I can't convince Evie? How will we help Bryson then?"

"Mother Gazina has a way—he's not the first child to visit the Fae—but the process takes nine days. Besides, if you can convince Evie to return... there is much to discuss."

"What I don't understand," Pa began, "is why Bryson was with you in the first place. All Jaria said was that you were both in the cave."

"I followed Jaria to the Fae. And Bryson followed me." My explanation sounded foolish. "He thought I was playing a game, and I didn't even know he was there until it was too late—" That wasn't quite true. "I could have stopped him, but I asked him to help me follow Jaria instead."

"But why did you go to the Fae?" Stepma pressed. "They don't like unexpected visitors, especially you—" she stopped.

Pa shook his head. "Jaria is the intermediary."

"I didn't believe Jaria was telling me everything." My accusation felt empty without evidence.

"They made her the intermediary for a reason," Pa said.

"Maybe if someone finally told me why I can't meet the Fae, I wouldn't have done it." I pulled my wrist from Stepma's grasp. "Besides, you are hiding something from me too."

Stepma sighed. "I should have told you this morning."

"Told me what?"

Stepma looked to Pa.

"Sit back down," Pa said.

I hadn't even realized I was standing. I settled in the chair. Finally, they would tell me everything. Only now that the time had come, it didn't seem worth the cost.

"Please don't think the worst of us. We did everything in love." Pa's voice carried unexpected gravity.

"Of course—I love you. You're my Pa."

"I guess that's where we start." Pa held my gaze. "Alice, I'm not your father."

"What? No."

"Maybe that's not right. I'm your parent—I raised you, I love you like Bryson. But I'm related to you as much as Sarene is."

I looked at Stepma. She nodded in agreement with his words. Pa still studied me with stiff intensity, and I wondered if his eyes were watering from rage. There could be no other explanation. Pa didn't cry.

He squeezed my shoulder. "I love you very much. I'm so proud to have raised you, but I'm not biologically related to you."

I struggled to understand this. "Is Evie my mother?"

"Yes."

"Then who is my father?"

Pa swallowed and opened his mouth, but he didn't speak.

"A human," Stepma said. "His name is Ash."

I repeated the name to myself, finding it foreign. But maybe, somewhere, in a distant memory... I'd possibly heard that name. *Ash.*

Stepma continued, "Evie met him while collecting information for the Fae. The boundary normally repels humans, but sometimes certain people can walk a little closer."

I recalled Mark's uncanny ability to appear near the boundary. Was he like Ash? My imagination began running with the idea. I struggled to imagine the scene where Evie had shown herself to Ash.

"And so... they met," I concluded.

"And so, they fell in love," Pa corrected. "As her friend, she told me about meeting Ash. Later she'd tell me how they'd talk for hours. I warned her, but Evie... Evie is passionate and sometimes rash. Eventually, she confided that she was pregnant. With you."

"With me." I understood his words but struggled to comprehend their full meaning. My dad was human? "But that's not possible! I look Bigfoot! Shouldn't I look more human?"

"The Fae changed your appearance when you were born. I was there," Stepma said. "Evie gave birth to you inside the Fae cave. Queen Avilana orchestrated the spell as Mother Gazina and I cared for Evie and you."

I tried to imagine it: Evie giving birth in that clammy cave with only Mother Gazina and Stepma to witness that her child was... a half-breed. I visualized Avilana overseeing it all and shivered.

Stepma pointed to my pendant. "Avilana bewitched your crystal. I don't know how the magic works, but the stone separates your human and Bigfoot essences, making it possible for you to look like either."

"But I can't appear as I actually am," I realized. I clutched the stone. "What did I look like when I was born?"

Stepma's gaze grew distant in recollection. "I suppose you were less furry than a Bigfoot babe? It's hard to say. You were a newborn and Avilana finished the spell within minutes of your birth."

"So neither of my bodies are real." The revelation

made me feel empty. I'd come to terms with acting like a human, but apparently, I was pretending with my entire identity.

"No matter what you look like, you're still you," Pa said. "You're frustratingly curious, whatever body you're in." He laughed, trying to joke.

I smiled weakly.

"Why were you there?" I asked Stepma, suddenly doubting everything I had once believed to be true. Was she more than she seemed to be? "And when did you and Pa—Caiman—"

"You will still call me Pa."

I nodded and looked to Stepma.

"As I said, I visited the Fae as a child," she began. "I had an aptitude for magic, but Evie was chosen as the apprentice."

"That's unfortunate." I believed Stepma would have been a good Mother.

She waved away my apology. "It's a long time ago, and I never would have had Pa or you or Bryson in my life any other way." It went unsaid that service for the Fae may have a higher cost than family. Jaria and Evie had shown that.

"Is that how you met pa?" I asked. "Did Evie connect you?"

Stepma nodded. "I was jealous of Evie and followed her around for a time. Not my best decision but..." She shrugged. "But between that and my magical instincts, I was trusted to help with your birth."

I turned to Pa. "You became mates with Evie to hide her pregnancy?"

"You make it sound worse than it was..." he replied. "But yes. I wanted a family and already knew Evie's secret. Since we were already friends, it seemed like a perfect solution."

"You never had a romantic relationship with Evie?"

He laughed and cleared his throat. "No."

Stepma chuckled.

I looked from one to the other, trying not to gape. "What happened between you two?"

"Well, Evie introduced us," Stepma began. "Naturally, we had seen each other from a distance, but it wasn't until Evie's pregnancy that we started talking and..." She looked to Pa. "I was attracted to you from the start."

"Me too," he replied. "But neither of us could handle another secret. We didn't want to hide a relationship."

Stepma nodded, and he reached for her hand and squeezed it. They really were sweet together.

I struggled to align this new information with my childhood memories. It seemed impossible that Stepma had already been connected to my family, that she had been there before I was born. She had carried my secret.

Pa continued, "When Evie disappeared—I still can't believe she's alive." He shook his head. "We did what we could to help you."

I nodded. They had done so much for me. They'd raised me, loved me as their own.

And in return, I had taken their child to the Fae. Maybe Bryson wasn't related to me like I'd believed, but he was my baby brother. The one I'd sworn to protect.

Tears welled up in my eyes, and I tried to blink them away. I wiped my face with my hand, hoping the gesture passed as fatigue. Stepma smiled at me.

"Thank you." My words sounded raspy. "Thank

you for being my parents."

Pa patted my hand, and Stepma held my shoulder. I allowed a few of the tears to fall. With their release, exhaustion took hold.

I yawned, my mouth opening wide despite my efforts to hold it back. It was a very late night. I had more questions, but everything they explained was struggling to settle within me. It seemed impossible to articulate anything else.

Our silence expanded.

"I should go to bed," I finally admitted. "Tomorrow's going to be a big day."

"It will be," Stepma agreed.

I stood and hugged each of them.

Then I climbed the ladder, too numb to notice my complaining knee. I crawled into the empty loft and lay down in Bryson's bed. Sleep shifted over me...

And maybe it was a dream, but I may have heard Pa talking downstairs. "You're the one who understood Evie's vision for Alice. Help me to help her."

The words brought more questions that I failed to grasp, but maybe they'd never been said at all.

Chapter 17

It was dark when I woke. And despite my attempts to return to sleep, anticipation stirred within me.

There was work to do.

Soft snores sounded from downstairs, but otherwise, silence. I climbed down the ladder, discovering that while my knee was stiff, it would take my weight.

I left without saying goodbye. There was nothing more to say. At this point, Evie could answer my remaining questions. Besides, I would regret stirring them.

The wind had died down, but it was drizzling. The water collected on my outer fur as I trudged past the farmland, making my way to the forest.

I crossed the boundary and shifted into my human form, thankful my transformed outfit included a raincoat—human skin was worse in the rain than Bigfoot fur. I continued walking, deep in thought, struggling to absorb this fresh perspective of who I was.

My human body wasn't the Fae illusion that I had assumed. Instead, it was as real as my Bigfoot appearance. Neither showed the truth, so did it really matter what I looked like?

Regardless of my form, I still made my own decisions. However I appeared, I was still me. Everyone else would judge me differently for my appearance—Bigfoot or human—but I was always Alice.

The full moon still hung in the sky, nearing the horizon and casting the house in its glow. I stepped inside, surprised to discover that the lights were already on. "Jaria?"

She sat on the couch, curled up in a blanket. Her favorite cartoon movie, *The Centaur Who Saw the Stars,* played on the TV. She turned to me, startled.

"Sorry, it's—" I checked the clock. "Five in the morning. I didn't think you'd be awake. But I couldn't sleep either."

She clutched a mug of coffee to her chest. Since discovering the beverage, she'd become obsessed. It was far too bitter for me.

The air carried the scent of the perfume. A fresh application. "It smells nice," I said.

She glared at me.

"I'm really sorry." Now that we were talking, I struggled to find words. "And thank you."

"Thank you?"

"You don't have to come to Aldertown with me. I made this mistake, but you're still helping me—even when you have every right to push me away. You make everything easier for me, and I take advantage of it."

Her eyes widened.

"I'm sorry. And thank you," I concluded.

I waited a long moment, holding my breath, hoping she'd speak soon. The movie started a musical number. Jaria paused the video and motioned toward the other side of the couch. "Do you want to sit down?"

"Yeah." I fumbled, first with the door and then my crystal as I shifted into my Bigfoot body. I perched on the couch cushion and prepared to speak.

"Alice, you're like a sister to me," Jaria said first.

I gulped, knowing it was true.

While I had Bryson, he was so much younger and that made our relationship fundamentally different. Jaria and I had spent much of our childhood together.

Evie had been like a second mother to her. And both of them had lived with the Fae. It was possible Evie had more in common with Jaria than me, her half-breed daughter.

"Secrecy was necessary when I lived with the Fae," Jaria continued. "Clearly, that's uncomfortable for you, and it's possible I've changed more than I know... But I am who I am, and I need you to accept that."

My throat tightened. I'd grieved for her when she'd vanished, and maybe that version of Jaria really was gone. It bothered me that I hadn't been there for her, and I couldn't understand why she wouldn't confide in me. I wanted to love her, but she kept pushing me away.

But now, I'd seen her trinkets under the waterfall. I understood that Bryson would be changed because of this. And I'd lost track of my own identity.

The Jaria I had once known couldn't return, but I wanted to know who she'd become.

"You're a sister to me too," I said. "And I'd like to be your friend again, if you'd give me that chance?"

She froze, and I wouldn't have blamed her for saying no. And if she didn't want to be friends, I'd have to accept that.

"Okay." She softened. "I need time, but we can try to be friends."

"Really?" I smiled. "I'll do better this time. No more following you into rabbit holes. I promise."

"And I promise to tell you everything that I know."

"Really?"

She rolled her eyes. "I can't exactly risk you doing something that foolish a second time."

Despite everything, I laughed. "I don't want to be foolish again either."

She took a sip of coffee and reached for the remote.

"Do you remember how Evie told the best stories?" I asked before she could press play.

"They were the best," Jaria replied.

"The stories were from books, weren't they?"

"I think so."

I paused. "Stepma and Pa told me something important last night. It's about... my father."

"I know," Jaria replied.

Despite our conversation, my temper was quick to flair. Of course she already knew.

"Mother Gazina explained last night," Jaria continued. "She said your parents were telling you too."

"Oh, all right."

"Are you okay?"

"Maybe? Okay enough? It's confusing."

Jaria nodded and pulled me toward her, inviting me to lean against her shoulder. I cuddled closer, and she pressed play. The cartoon characters sang their song.

Chapter 18

We finished the movie together. The sun still hadn't risen, but it would take several hours to reach Aldertown. Neither of us could hold still any longer, so it was time to leave.

Evie's business card was crammed into my desk drawer. I retrieved it and dialed the number, hesitating before starting the call.

It went to voicemail, so I sent her a text. *This is Alice. We need your help. Call me.*

Meanwhile, Jaria packed her satchel with various spellcasting supplies we hoped we wouldn't need. There was no time to prepare another persuasion spell.

We were relying on Evie to invite us into SEA, trusting her promise that we were welcome back. Besides, even if I was made persuasive, it was possible Dr. Oleski would see through it.

My hands shook as I searched the kitchen for food. I hoped Evie would call me back soon, prayed she would help us.

Nothing in the pantry looked good to me.

"Hey, Jaria," I called to her. "Can we stop by the market on our way through Piner? I'd like to pick up some breakfast."

"Are they open?" She settled a jar into her bag.

"I know Payton's working."

She studied me as she closed the satchel. "All right. I'd like some different food too."

I tried calling Evie a second time—no response—and we loaded into the Godparent Express. Flora started the car, and we began the quick journey into Piner.

The parking lot of Fresher Food Market was nearly empty. Fortunately, the open sign was lit.

"I'll stay here," Jaria said. "Can you buy me a croissant? And something with caffeine."

"Sure." I pulled my wallet from my backpack and stepped from the car.

The store still smelled of cleaning supplies. An employee greeted me as I entered, and I walked to the bakery at the rear.

Payton worked at a back table, packaging fresh bread.

"Can I help you?" another of the employees asked.

"Actually—"

"Alice!" Payton looked up, her eyes bright, first with recognition and then confusion. "Why are you here? It's so early."

"We were driving through and needed food. Thought I'd say hi."

Payton raised an eyebrow. She turned toward her coworker, and they chatted as I selected a few croissants.

"Alice, let me finish this," Payton said. "I'll take my break in a few minutes?"

I agreed and began searching for the canned coffee beverage Jaria liked. I had just finished checking out when Payton reached the front of the store.

"I've got fifteen minutes. What's going on?" she

asked as we walked to the empty cafe at the front of the store. We claimed our favorite table in the back corner.

She unwrapped a breakfast sandwich. "Want any?"

"Not right now."

"You're not interested in food? Something really is bothering you."

I surprised myself by laughing. "It's been a weird night."

She eyed the coffee, knowing it wasn't for me. "I assume your plan to follow Jaria didn't work out?"

"Not at all," I began and then lowered my voice as I explained what had happened. It hadn't been a full day since I'd last seen Payton, but everything had shifted. I had a brother to save, an estranged mother to visit, and a new identity to understand.

"So now you're part-human?" Payton asked.

"Apparently?"

"Weird plot twist."

"I know."

"And now we're heading to Aldertown." I shook the bag of croissants. "Jaria's waiting in the car, and I've got food for the road."

Payton took a bite and chewed. "Can I..." She swallowed. "Can I come with you?"

"What?" She'd never ridden in the Godparent Express, never been to the house. Jaria had insisted we keep it that way. "Don't you have work to do?"

"Most of the hard stuff is done... and my coworker owes me one."

"Won't your mom be frustrated?"

"My problem, not yours. So, what do you think?" She sat taller. "Can I come?"

"I'm not sure Jaria will approve..."

"I'll bring cookies! There's a bag of day-olds that'll be delicious."

I considered, pretending I could tell her no. But I liked the idea of Payton joining us. Besides, Jaria would appreciate the cookies...

"Okay," I said.

She squealed with excitement. "I'll be right back. Let me clear this up."

Payton practically ran to the bakery while I stared at the sandwich she'd left behind. A few days ago, I would have been thrilled by the prospect of Payton coming with us, but after having Bryson follow me the night before, I wasn't so sure.

What if Payton was hurt?

"Let's go." Payton wore her coat and carried a bag of cookies.

"Are you sure—" I began, but her smile was so big.

"Am I sure... this is the best cookie?" She studied the bag. "I chose chocolate chip because it seemed like the safest option, but does Jaria like something else? Does she dislike chocolate?"

"The cookies are great. But..." I sighed. "This might be dangerous. Bryson is with the Fae because he followed me. I don't want anything to happen to you."

Payton rewrapped her sandwich. "Come on Alice, I've already taken the day off. It's spring break, let's do something." She pulled my hand and led me to the parking lot.

"Let me go talk to Jaria." I ran to the Godparent Express and opened the backseat door. The coffee was plucked from my hands, appearing to float in the air.

"Are those the croissants?" Jaria asked.

"Yes." I handed her the bag. "And—"

"You brought Payton," Jaria said, presumably looking out the window. "I thought you promised you'd check with me before doing anything foolish."

"I am. I'm checking with you now. It's just... I came here because I needed to talk with her, and we did talk. And she's decided that she wants to come with us."

"That is absolutely—"

"I know. But what do you think?"

Payton opened the other backseat door and shoved herself into the seat before anyone could stop her.

"I brought cookies!" She waved the bag in the air. "They were baked yesterday, but I swear they're still good."

Jaria growled but didn't say no. The bag floated, opened itself, and one of the cookies was lifted upward, only to crumble and dissipate as Jaria ate it.

"It's good," Jaria admitted.

I grabbed a cookie and took a bite I could barely taste.

"Jaria." Payton stared at the place where the cookie had vanished. "I understand that we didn't start on the right page. It's okay if you don't like me... but can you give me this chance? You can drop me off with my family in Aldertown if you prefer, but let me ride down with you. I want the chance to know you better."

An icy silence greeted her request. I assumed Jaria was figuring out how to say no, but the car revved into life as Flora turned the key.

"Promise me that, if it becomes necessary, you'll do as I say." Jaria said.

"Promise." Payton buckled her seatbelt and handed another cookie into the open air. "Girls' trip!"

she cheered.

Presumably Jaria rolled her eyes, but even if she did, she still accepted the second cookie.

Chapter 19

Payton chatted for most of the ride to Aldertown. She had to be as tired as we were, but she didn't act it. Her enthusiasm became contagious.

Jaria even laughed at Payton's jokes, and Payton's charm began eroding Jaria's animosity.

That made me smile. Payton was someone really special—anybody who made Jaria laugh had to be. They were so different from each other. Payton's bright cheer and transparent disposition contrasted with Jaria completely. I never imagined their re-introduction could go smoothly—but they proved me wrong.

As Jaria continued to question Payton about different types of cookies, I tried to call Evie again. No response. I checked my text messages. No reply. I tapped my fingers against the phone, but still... nothing.

The drive went on. And despite everything, I yawned and my eyelids drooped. I stretched my feet out, and at long last, I closed my eyes.

I may have drifted in and out of sleep, stirring now and then to check my phone and confirm that nothing had changed.

Jaria and Payton seemed able to talk the entire drive. Even in their company, I found the solitude I needed.

In my sleepiness, I found the stillness that had evaded me the night before. And maybe I wouldn't achieve understanding, but I began to take steps toward clarity.

Last fall, when I'd entered the human world, my life had changed completely. Over the months, I'd settled into a routine, and maybe it wasn't perfect, but it felt familiar.

And now everything would change again.

The shift seemed bigger than Evie or Bryson, larger than the prospect of Payton befriending Jaria. The perception I had of myself was incomplete. For the second time in less than a year, my identity had shifted.

The narratives I had constructed about myself were wrong. Evie had chosen to stay away. Pa wasn't my father, and I hadn't kept my promise to keep Bryson safe.

And—as weird as it sounded—I was grieving for the person I thought I had been.

My childhood fantasy of my ma as a lone Bigfoot, desperately working her way home, was complete nonsense. My recollection of Pa and Ma as a normal couple was a misinterpreted memory.

My belief that I was a Bigfoot wasn't even true.

Instead, I was a half-breed. A mutt—a monster.

I shivered, trying to push the word from my mind. *Monster.* But it ran with my imagination. What did I really look like? Was I a furry human or a bald Bigfoot? Neither prospect excited me.

I was still me. Under the skin, I would always be Alice. I repeated that to myself, hoping that I was right about that, that the words *I'm still Alice* were even true.

I woke to the sound of tinny music. Groggily I stirred, sluggishly lifting a heavy hand to pick up my phone. But when I saw, *Call from Evie,* adrenaline kicked me into motion. I panicked and answered the call.

"'Lo," I said, my stiff tongue lolling in my mouth. I cleared my throat. "Hello."

"Alice? It's Evie. Are you okay?"

What a question. "Um..."

"We're nearly there," Jaria whispered. "We're twenty minutes away."

I replied to Evie, "We need to talk. I'm already on my way to see you. I'm twenty minutes away. Can you tell the front desk to let me in?"

"What's going on?"

"Uh..." I rubbed my eyes with my free hand.

"Are you safe?"

"I'm safe. Yes. But Bryson—"

"Who is Bryson?" she asked.

"My half-brother—I guess he's my step-brother? I don't know." My brain seemed sluggish. "It's been a long night."

"It was a full moon."

"It definitely was."

"I'm going to assume the Fae are involved."

"They most certainly are."

The line was quiet another moment before she replied, "I'll let the front desk know. Let's talk when you get here."

"Thank you," I breathed as she hung up the phone.

Chapter 20

By the time we reached SEA's parking lot, I had shaken the worst of the grogginess from my body. Unfortunately, anxiety took its place.

Dr. Oleski waited, seemingly alone, on a bench outside the building. He seemed to be talking to himself, so I guessed Evie sat nearby, cloaked in her invisibility.

I studied him and swallowed. Hopefully, he wouldn't hold my earlier deception against me. Even if my conversation with Evie went well, he had the power to make this journey difficult.

I turned to the back seat. An empty bag that had once held cookies lay abandoned in the middle. Maybe it was their first step toward friendship.

"Go ahead," Jaria encouraged.

Stretching and sighing, I opened the car door. I stood, thankful that my knee didn't buckle.

Payton stepped from the car and slapped my back, just like in a volleyball game. Her encouragement lightened my steps. While I couldn't see Jaria, my fingertips twitched as her icy chill passed over them.

Together, we approached Dr. Oleski.

"Who's this?" Dr. Oleski pointed to Payton. He addressed the empty seat next to him. "I gave clearance for Alice to enter."

I scanned the space he'd addressed, assuming Evie was there. "This is my friend, Payton. She knows what I am."

Dr. Oleski frowned, his brows creasing.

Evie spoke from the empty seat. "It's nice to meet you, Payton."

Payton's eyes grew gigantic, and a giggle escaped her lips. "Oh wow. It's nice to meet you too."

Dr. Oleski sighed. I held back my laughter, wondering how he'd react if he knew Jaria was there too.

"Can we talk?" I asked Evie. "Preferably somewhere I can see you."

"We can go into the forest," she replied.

The trees were thick, and we wouldn't need to walk far to be out of sight. "Okay," I agreed.

Dr. Oleski huffed, still staring at Payton. "Are you sure that's wise?"

"If Alice trusts Payton..." Evie said.

He shifted uncomfortably.

"Is Jaria here?" Evie asked.

"I am." Jaria replied.

Dr. Oleski jumped at the sound of her voice and looked toward the spot where she stood. "Another invisible Bigfoot?"

"My name is Jaria. I accompanied Alice on Monday."

Dr. Oleski glared at Evie, shook his head, and sighed. "Fine. Let's go."

He led us to a trail that wrapped around the building. The path wiggled deeper into the forest.

"What's going on?" Evie asked as we walked. She must have fallen into step beside me, and I heard the thunk of her staff as she walked.

"I'll explain soon—it's easier if I see you. Is it actually safe here?"

"I avoid visibility near the main entrance, but it's safe everywhere. After all, I'm not SEA's only supernatural guest, and most of them live in the forest."

"What does supernatural mean? Like the Fae?" I asked.

"Among others."

I didn't ask her to clarify. There were plenty of myths that seemed possible: from mermaids and centaurs to dragons and angels. Who was I to say what was real?

As we walked, I kept my eyes toward the trees. If I paid better attention, maybe I'd see something interesting.

The path led us to a small meadow. Fallen tree trunks had been cut into makeshift benches, and a cold firepit lay at their center.

Evie removed her pendant and appeared beside me. She began tying the necklace around her wrist, a motion Jaria had performed countless times.

Following suit, Jaria materialized beside Payton. Dr. Oleski held back his gasp and sighed it out. His gaze passed from Jaria's crystal to Evie's, and finally, toward mine.

He pointed at my pendant. "Evie says you can appear Bigfoot too? Can you—Forgive me. I'm curious—"

I removed the necklace and transformed into my Bigfoot form.

Dr. Oleski considered me with scientific curiosity, but I didn't give him my attention. I only had eyes for Evie.

Evie took in my Bigfoot appearance, this one

more familiar to her than my human form had been. She reached a hand toward me, and I gripped her forearm in return. Not quite an embrace, but it was enough for me.

Evie tugged me aside. "Did you want to talk privately?"

Relieved she had spoken first, I nodded and followed her to the other side of the meadow.

Dr. Oleski's frown somehow deepened, but Evie gave him a reassuring grin. He shrugged.

I looked at Payton and Jaria.

"We'll be fine," Payton said, pulling out her phone. "Besides, there's a video I wanted to show Jaria, but it wouldn't load in the car."

Jaria didn't seem quite as comfortable, but she sat down on a log bench. Payton settled beside her, placing her phone between them.

Dr. Oleski scowled at the device. "I should confiscate that... Just please, no photos or video."

"Not my first time around Bigfoots." Payton gave him a thumbs up without looking at him. She pressed play.

"I'm sorry," Evie said as we reached the other side. "You caught me by surprise the other day, and I didn't handle it the best."

Then, somehow, I chuckled. "I'm not proud of how I handled it either."

Suddenly she was hugging me. Part of me objected, but familiarity stirred too.

She wasn't everything I wanted her to be, but we still shared many things. Maybe she didn't express her love the way I wanted, but I could stop questioning if her love was there.

The last of my fear faded as we stepped back from our embrace. While I couldn't control how she responded, I needed a steady mind to explain myself to her.

"Stepma—Sarene—and Pa have a son. His name is Bryson," I began.

"Sarene and Caiman are together? And they raised you?" She seemed relieved when I nodded. "I had always hoped that—After I left—" She shook her head. "What's happened to Bryson?"

"Last night I followed Jaria into the Fae cave, and Bryson followed me."

"I'm guessing the Fae didn't like that."

"Not at all. They called me unpleasant." I frowned.

She snickered. "They've called you that since the day you were born."

"It's not very nice of them."

"It's nothing personal. You're not a typical Bigfoot—"

"It's because I'm part-human, isn't it?"

She seemed relieved that I'd said it. "You know then? About... your father."

"I learned last night, thank you very much."

Evie shifted. "I see. Well, the Fae dislike humans because they block their magic. I'm not exactly sure what you do to them, but clearly it's unpleasant."

The explanation didn't actually make me feel better.

"What happened after you and Bryson entered the cave?" she asked.

"We danced. And for a few minutes, it was nice. But then Jaria poured water on me and cleared the Faerydust. Queen Avilana arrived and..." I shook my head.

"And they already had Bryson?" she asked.

I nodded. "Queen Avilana said if you talk with her, he'll be released. Mother Gazina says there are other ways to bring him back, but it's fastest if you return with us."

She stayed silent for several long seconds. "I understand."

"Then you'll come back with us?"

"The Fae don't want me, not as I've become." She sat down on a log bench, staring at me for a long second. "The shape of your human face is like your father... Did you know?"

"How would I know that?" I snapped. I shook my head; staying calm was so hard. "What happened to him?"

"Hmm, how to begin... What do you know of Jaria's training?"

"Jaria? What's she got to do with anything?"

"We were trained in the same way. The Fae cave is where my story begins."

"She doesn't like talking about it," I said. "But I know she started training two years ago and returned last Summer Solstice—the same night I received my crystal. I know she learned Fae magic, studied humans, and prepared my human identity." Truthfully, Jaria had done many things to make my deception possible.

"I did some of that." Evie nodded. "I spent my days sleeping behind the waterfall and my nights studying magic. Once I was ready, I began visiting Piner and learning about humans."

"And then met my father, *Ash*." His name still felt strange on my tongue. "You met him."

She nodded. "As I'm sure you've realized, the Fae hid the Bigfoot Village inside Evergreen National Forest. Ash worked as a park ranger."

"Where is he now?"

She twisted her hands around her staff. "Dead."

126

My mind reeled.

Did I grieve a man I only recently learned existed? Or was I disappointed that I wouldn't know him? It was possible that I felt nothing, already too numb to respond to more information.

She continued, "He died the day I disappeared... Do you remember that tree, the one I took you to as a child? It's near the boundary."

I nodded. *My tree.* The one that had fallen a few months ago when I had climbed it, running from my own fears.

"When you were young, I took you there so he could watch you. He stayed hidden behind the bushes—but he could see you." Evie smiled at the recollection.

"You brought him through the boundary?" I didn't know it was possible.

"It's one of the crystal's many abilities, but I never took him any further into the village."

My anger swelled. I could have met my father! He had seen me, but I'd never have the chance to meet him. "How did he die?"

"There was an accident." She clicked her claws against her staff. "The Fae asked me to begin negotiations with SEA, and Ash accompanied me. It was our first big meeting, and I made the mistake of entering it invisible. But as the meeting was about to start, I decided it would be easier to communicate if I could be seen and removed my pendant.

"There was a younger park ranger with us. When I appeared, she thought I was a bear or... something." She shook her head and tapped her injured leg. "She shot me, and Ash tried to stop her. The second bullet killed your father."

I swallowed, stifling my urge to interrupt.

127

"I don't remember much of what happened next, but I've been told SEA restrained and erased the memory from the ranger. Then they brought me here for surgery, and I stayed to recover. It wasn't just my leg that needed to heal. Losing Ash—I can't expect you to understand. I'm not proud this happened—losing him broke everything inside me. At first, I had every intention of returning to the village..."

"But you didn't."

She sighed. "Caiman and Sarene were in love, but I stood in their way. As for myself, I never fit in with the rest of the village. For your sake, I should have fought for you and found a better solution, but it seemed impossible. I was so tired after Ash died. And..." She looked away. "And I believed Sarene could be a better mother than me."

I stilled my tongue, biting back the temptation to agree with her.

"As I recovered, I began using the internet. While researching for the Fae, I discovered I enjoyed reading. Over the years, I had borrowed a few books for myself, but I'd rarely had the opportunity to read for hours.

"As my leg healed, I needed distraction. The internet gave me a way to order books and post reviews without anybody suspecting I was Bigfoot. First, I worked to fill a void, but then it was my passion... My leg healed, but I didn't return home."

My throat was dry with anger, but I nodded without interrupting. Now wasn't the time to lose my temper.

"Alice, I'm sorry. There is nothing I can say that will undo the selfishness of my choice. I stayed away for me, but I deprived you. I'm not proud to confess this. I haven't acted in ways that mothers are supposed to... but that's the truth."

I sat next to her and worked to process the information. Logically, I listed the facts—but all I felt was a numb grief, an emptiness filled by the possibilities she had taken from me.

It was impossible to keep this in perspective. All things considered, I had enjoyed a secure childhood, especially considering my unusual parentage. There had been the trauma of my ma's disappearance, yes, but Stepma and Pa had raised me as if I was their own.

More emotions began brewing in me, accumulating until they became a chaos so vast no single feeling rose above the others. I swallowed and narrowed my focus to the conversation at hand.

"Will you help me with Bryson?" I asked. "He's the reason I'm here."

"Alice—" She thudded her staff against the ground. "Of course I'll go." She sighed. "I can't begin to say how sorry I am—"

I shook my head. "Don't."

"I understand if you can't treat me like a mother, but I would like the chance to know you better."

The words knocked at my heart, but I couldn't open up. Trust takes time, and right now, there was no space for her. Instead, I swallowed and looked around the clearing. Dr. Oleski, Jaria, and Payton were chatting, finally at ease.

I cleared my throat. "If your mind is made up, we should go to the village. Thank you for your assistance." With my anger carefully contained, all I could do was state the facts.

Chapter 21

We waited for Evie in the parking lot. She and Dr. Oleski had returned to her rooftop cabin so she could pack a bag. And though she'd seemed confident in her decision, there was a part of me expecting that she'd stay in her cabin.

Dr. Oleski had been surprised to hear Evie would, at least temporarily, be leaving. But he'd done nothing to convince her to stay. She truly had been there voluntarily, and the knowledge both relieved and irritated me.

The three of us chatted—debating who should sit where for the return drive and concluding that, regardless of configuration, it would be a crowded car. Through our conversation, I was relieved to see Payton's and Jaria's easygoing interaction.

All it took was an adventure.

Dr. Oleski stepped from the building, holding the door open as Evie passed through behind him. He carried a duffle bag and loaded it into the trunk.

"Alice." He turned to me and studied my face like he was looking for something. "I wish we could have met under different circumstances. But as Evie will testify, SEA exists to ease relations between humans and entities like Bigfoots. If there is anything I can do—" He handed me a business card. "Don't hesitate to ask."

"Thanks." I accepted the card. A continued relationship with SEA seemed like an inevitability. "We should talk soon."

He nodded.

I opened the front door. "Evie will be most comfortable up here."

"Thanks," she said.

"Evie, I'm..." He sighed and stood tall. "I'll miss our chats. It might be selfish of me, but I hope you'll be back soon."

"Carl, thanks for everything. And don't worry, I'll see you soon." Evie closed the door.

Her words sparked my anger—she had promised her return so casually when she had never returned to me—but I swallowed my objection.

"Thanks for all your help, Dr. Oleski," I said, crawling into the backseat with Payton and Jaria.

Flora started the car and finally—*finally*—we were off.

I snuggled deeper into my seat. Even if I was crammed next to Jaria, at least we were headed home. Evie was with us, and if everything went according to plan, Bryson would be returned to my family by sunset.

But still, I shifted, unable to contain my curiosity. "What is your relationship with Dr. Oleski? You called him Carl."

My question was greeted by silence, and then, thankfully, Payton burst out laughing.

"Alice!" Jaria sounded grumpy. "We've barely left! You can't—"

"It's fine," Evie interrupted. "We're friends. He was my first contact with SEA, and... he was there when Ash died."

Oh. "So he knew my father."

"Yes."

That quieted me, but Jaria had more questions. So, Evie explained it all again, how my father had died. This time, she offered more details, like how he'd rushed to protect her, how he'd died in her arms.

Upon hearing it the second time, I found I could wonder... Did Evie have a photo of him? How had they met? And what was the story of their unexpected romance?

There were more practical questions too. Besides SEA, who knew Bigfoots were real? And how much about the village did SEA know? I wondered what happened to the ranger who'd shot her, the one who'd been brainwashed into forgetting.

The radio switched songs as we reached the fence. The gate rose, and we drove forward. If Evie hesitated, I didn't see it.

"The car's impressive," she said. "Something like this would have made my life much easier."

"Uh... thanks," Jaria replied.

"You must be more advanced in magic than me. Even at my best, I don't think I could have done this."

"It seems I have an aptitude for it. The way it stretches the brain and twists reality. It comes easily for me."

It was odd to hear Jaria hesitate about her abilities. She always seemed eager to complain about how much work was required of her. She was justifying her efforts to me, and I was an unappreciative audience.

But Evie was impressed. She asked more questions, and while I followed their early exchange, the conversation diverged into concepts like abstract reality, reorganizational entropy, and cerebral mimicry.

Payton looked at me, silently asking if I understood any of it.

Not at all. I shook my head, trying not to laugh.

They continued talking and connecting. Jealousy rose from my stomach, but I managed to swallow it. My connection with Evie was rocky and messy, not the smooth relationship Jaria had.

But Jaria needed Evie too. Maybe Evie was my mother, but she'd helped raise Jaria. They also shared their experiences with the Fae.

Living with the Fae was one adventure I wouldn't experience—especially considering my 'unpleasantness.' But maybe, if my jealousy didn't get in the way, Evie could help Jaria heal. Jaria needed that.

When all this was over, I decided I'd give Jaria a proper gift—something more genuine than the perfume. But for now, I wouldn't interrupt their discussion.

"Hey Payton, where should we drop you off?" Jaria asked as we reached the outskirts of Piner.

"You can take me home," Payton replied. "It's—"

"I know where it is," Jaria cut her off.

"I guess you do."

"Actually," Evie began, "I thought Payton might come with us. We could use her help."

"Her help?" I squeaked. Glancing at Payton, I discovered the idea excited her.

"You think she can help with the Faerydust?" Jaria asked.

"It'll help Bryson acclimate faster," Evie answered.

Payton looked at me for guidance, but I didn't understand what they were talking about. I objected, "We can't just take a human across the boundary—" But Evie had taken my father into Bigfoot lands. "What do you mean, acclimate?"

"By the time we reach him, Bryson will have spent a night and a day with the Fae," Evie began. "That's long enough for Faerydust to become sticky. The waterfall can help, but..."

"But contact with a human is faster," Jaria concluded. "All Payton needs to do is touch Bryson. That'll force even the most stubborn of Faerydust to leave him."

"All she has to do is hike across Bigfoot land and reach the Fae cave," I said. "Because that can't possibly go wrong."

Yet Payton's expression remained hopeful. She always wanted more from my adventure.

"Can I really help Bryson?" Payton asked.

"He'll be fine either way," Jaria replied, "but this will ease his transition."

"But what if someone sees her?" I asked. "Then they'll ask questions and... I don't even know what'll happen."

"I'm the apprentice to the Mother," Jaria said. "And Evie is—well, her reappearance will confuse anyone who recognizes her. Besides, if we keep to the outskirts, nobody will see us. And even if someone crosses our path, I can cast a glamor over Payton."

"Alice, what do you think?" Payton asked. We were approaching Payton's house and needed to decide. Excitement and anticipation danced in her expression.

"You want to go?" I asked.

She nodded.

"And it'll help Bryson?"

"Yes," Evie confirmed. "And we'll keep her safe."

"Then if Payton wants to, she should could come with us." I said aloud, wishing that speaking the words made me feel more excited about this—a better friend wouldn't have been so afraid. "No reason to break up the girl's trip quite yet."

So we drove past Piner, continuing deeper into the mountains, and despite the sinking sensation in my stomach, I didn't ask Jaria to turn the car around.

Chapter 22

Flora parked the car inside the garage and closed the door behind us. Unable to delay another moment, Jaria appeared beside me, sighing with relief. "Feels good to be me again."

"It's safe?" Evie asked.

"I've enchanted the house. Only those I've allowed can approach," Jaria answered.

Evie became visible and shook out her fur. "That's better."

"We should hurry to Northridge." My car-ride lethargy was turning into urgency.

It was time to retrieve Bryson. And then, once we had him, Payton could return to Piner. And then... there was something else, something I was forgetting. But what was it—

"Let's go." Jaria pushed her hip against mine. "Alice, can you open the door?"

"Yeah." My knee was still stiff, but it took my weight without complaint. I watched Evie step from the car with careful precision, and my discomfort seemed frivolous by comparison.

We entered the house, lingering long enough to reset and refresh. Food and bathroom? Check. Jaria and I feeling embarrassed by how messy everything was? Double-check.

The clutter didn't give the first impression I had hoped for, but thankfully, Evie saw past it.

"Jaria did this?" She asked while we waited for the bathroom.

"She did an excellent job." I tried to view the cluttered living room as Evie might see it, realizing how the mess made it look like a home.

Jaria and Evie donned their visibility for the short hike to the boundary as the sun peaked from behind the clouds. It wasn't raining or cold. It could even have been a pleasant day for a hike.

The perimeter was as benign as ever, and I shifted my body, letting it catch in the light. It flashed in reply, golden and glinting.

But Payton hugged herself with her arms.

"What's wrong?" I asked.

She shook her head. "Every nerve of my body wants to go back."

"It's the boundary. Let me invite you in," Jaria explained. Then she continued, her voice becoming manganous, "We ask, honorable Fae, that Payton may enter these lands. I will be her guardian." She paused. "Now Payton, it's your turn. Tell the Fae you'll behave."

Payton shivered. "Hon-honorable Fae." She cleared her throat. "I will do no harm."

My knees buckled as I watched. Payton looked pale...

But as the words settled, she stood a little straighter and dropped her arms to her side.

"Better?" Evie asked.

"Better." Payton contemplated the boundary. "Now I can cross?"

"Go ahead."

I offered Payton my hand, but she didn't need it.

She marched forward as though she'd never doubted. While I wouldn't question her courage, I hoped her faith wasn't misplaced.

My body shifted to my Bigfoot form as Jaria and Evie materialized nearby. Payton wrung her hands and chewed her lip.

Evie's gaze followed the fallen tree, its corpse stretching across the perimeter. She frowned, her brow furrowed.

The tree marked my safe space, this location had comforted me throughout my childhood—and once it had been Evie's place, where she had helped Ash to see me from afar—but it was also where I'd grieved for her, where I'd gone for solace in the years since she'd left.

In time, I could learn to share the space with her. But not yet. For now, I turned to the path. We needed to keep moving.

Evie took the lead and set the pace. She moved slower than I could, but she was surprisingly fit. She must have hiked the trails around SEA, and I wondered which supernatural guests may have been her companions.

Evie had more questions to ask Jaria, and soon, they were walking side by side. Jaria updated Evie with the latest drama from the Fae court, and between the strange names and nuanced relationships, I quickly lost track of the conversation.

I fell into step beside Payton and opened my mouth, wanting to ask if she was okay, if she felt safe, but I never followed through. She had chosen this and wouldn't appreciate me questioning her. I chose to trust her judgment and wanted to show it. Besides, she seemed interested in listening to Jaria's updates on the Fae.

At long last, Evie and Jaria ran out of second-cousins of the Queen's general to discuss. For a time we were quiet, taking one step after another.

When we reached the halfway point, I looked to the sky. Dark gray clouds had gathered overhead, and I hoped it wouldn't rain.

Eventually, Evie spoke. "I'm impressed by what you two have accomplished."

I looked at Jaria, hoping she'd respond. She had made the house and bewitched the car; she'd enrolled me in high school and given me the tools to succeed. All I did was... complain, it seemed.

That wasn't entirely true. My grades were decent, and I'd learned to blend in with my human peers. But those contributions were rarely completed without a complaint.

Since the fall, I'd been frustrated with Jaria, convinced she was holding back vital information. And while she was discerning with what she told me, I no longer believed she was as deceptive as I had once thought.

Evie continued, "You've both grown so much since I left. I'm glad you've taken care of each other."

I wanted to laugh at her assumption that Jaria and I were on good terms. But Jaria turned around. She smiled at me and shrugged.

Maybe there was a sliver of truth to Evie's words.

The path widened, and Evie fell into step beside me. Payton ran forward to join Jaria.

"Did Alice tell you about *Goblins from Outer Space?*" Payton asked, and when Jaria said no, Payton began telling the story from the beginning.

Evie spoke, her voice so low only I could hear. "You must think the worst of me."

"N-No. Of course not! And I mean that..." I winced. "I think."

She chuckled, and I relaxed. While I didn't understand our new relationship, that relationship deserved a chance.

I continued, "Really, I am happy that you're here, in my life again. Only there is a lot for me to think about. But right now, you're here because I asked you to come. That's enough."

"That's more than I deserve."

I didn't disagree. We took a few more steps. Northridge wasn't far now, but the rest of our journey was uphill. Even my breathing was becoming labored.

"You've accomplished so much," Evie continued.

"Jaria's the one with magic. It's mostly her."

"You befriended Payton. And Jaria tells me you joined the volleyball team."

"That's not the same as creating a house and generating an identity for Alice Turner."

"Magic won't be enough. We need diplomacy too," Evie mused.

I didn't quite grasp her meaning. "Jaria's never told me why I need to learn how to be human. I'm not even sure she understands why. But I've started to assume that's why, isn't it? I'm needed for diplomacy?"

"Jaria might not know everything about the fading. When it comes to the topic, the Fae are aloof, so it took me ages to understand... But long story short, the Fae are leaving."

My breath stuck in my throat. "Leaving? But the Crux, the boundary—"

"The village depends on the Fae's blessing," she agreed.

My brain began racing. If the Fae weren't there, the perimeter would fall and the Bigfoot would... We would have to live beside the humans. "Why?"

"As the natural world fades, so does their magic. They need to retreat to their kingdom elsewhere— and soon. Queen Avilana hoped to leave within a generation."

"No one said anything—"

"The Fae are not forthcoming about their weaknesses."

I chewed my lip. "So, when you first met SEA... You've been preparing for this."

She nodded. "Once, the Fae believed I'd be the Bigfoot ambassador. For years, I thought the burden of introducing ourselves to humankind rested on my shoulders. And then..."

"You became pregnant with me," I said for her.

"I didn't even realize Ash and I could conceive... But there you were: the perfect proof that our two kinds could intermingle."

I laughed. "I've been too busy worrying about my actual appearance to see it that way."

She didn't laugh with me. "The Fae chose you as the true ambassador before you were even born. While I've opened discussions with SEA, you inherited a responsibility I never wanted to give. And... I'm sorry."

I swallowed. Acting human had been like a game to me, an interesting challenge. However, if the Fae were leaving, my role was much more necessary than I'd imagined. Could I even be a good ambassador? What if I failed?

"When Caiman agreed to our arrangement," Evie

continued, "he made the Fae promise one thing."

"What?"

"If you don't want to do this, you don't have to. There will always be a place for you in the village."

I recalled how Pa had confronted Mother Gazina when I started using my powers, telling her I wasn't old enough. Yesterday, he'd offered to help me reunite with Daylen. While his methods confused me, I never questioned if he valued my happiness.

Only my happiness wasn't everything. "If the Fae's magic is fading, we need an ambassador. If it's not me—"

"If it's not you, we will find someone. Maybe it's still me," Evie said. "But this has to be your choice."

It was something I'd already chosen. And even though Evie and Pa were eager to give me alternatives, I couldn't turn away. And it wasn't just out of duty to my people—I couldn't imagine a future where I didn't see this through.

"I believe what I'm doing is important," I admitted.

"That's wonderful to hear, I'm sorry that—"

Evie tripped and caught herself.

I reached out to help. "You okay?"

She righted herself. "It's fine. I get clumsy when I'm tired. We're nearly there."

"Just a few more minutes."

I wondered what her life would look like if she returned to the village. Her limp wasn't an impossible hurdle, some Bigfoots had graver injuries, but she had adjusted to life with humans. Our lifestyle involved so much walking. She could live at SEA, but what if—

"What if Jaria added a room to the house?" I asked. "We've got books and internet. You can use the car to visit SEA."

Jaria looked back when I said her name. "Alice, what a brilliant idea! It'll probably take me a lunar month to add another wing, but it's possible." She looked to Evie. "If you'd like that sort of thing."

We turned the corner of the final switchback, and the circle of tree stumps entered our sights.

Evie grinned. "I'd love to have a room at the house."

Chapter 23

"Alice, you should stay here with Payton," Jaria said as she pulled the rabbit hole wider.

Payton's jaw gaped as the ground opened up, and she saw the underground tunnel. Despite everything she'd seen in movies, actual magic was pretty exciting.

"She's right," Evie agreed. "Jaria and I should handle this."

"But it's so interesting..." Payton crawled to the edge and peered into the cave.

"Don't." Jaria grabbed her shoulder. "It's enchanting, but trust me, you don't want to meet them. If they think Alice is unpleasant... Well, you're worse."

Payton sat on her heels.

"We'll be right back," Jaria promised. She snatched her crystal, dropped into the tunnel, and landed gracefully on the ground.

"See you soon!" Evie jumped after her, using her crystal to ease her own landing.

They walked away and out of sight. The hole shriveled up, becoming an uninteresting detail in the earth.

I sat on the closest stump, and Payton dropped on the one next to me. When they returned, I'd see

Bryson. My foot tapped with impatience.

We'd spent so much time in the car that I hadn't noticed how late it'd become. I searched for the sun, deciding it was somewhere behind a cloud. Sunset was maybe an hour away.

Friday at sunset. That rang a bell—

Mark. We were meeting at sunset!

How could I possibly go on a date? Both Payton and Bryson needed me!

What would Mark think if I didn't show up? I could explain on Monday... but that would be awkward. Besides, I also needed to ask about the girl at the movies.

I started clicking my claws against the stump.

"Alice?" Payton asked.

"Yeah?"

"Are you bothered that I came along?"

"It's not that—"

Payton continued, "This is the coolest thing that's ever happened to me, but I'm not sure you're okay with it."

Her observation stung because she was right. Showing her the house and taking her past the perimeter should have been exciting keystones of our relationship. But I certainly wasn't acting that way.

"This is special." I met her gaze but glanced away. I stood and paced. "But what if I fail to protect you?"

"Protect me?" She waved to the empty clearing around us. "From what?"

"From everything!" I didn't mean to shout.

"Jaria and Evie aren't worried."

"They have magic. I don't."

She scoffed.

"Besides," I continued. "I've already changed Bryson's life, and I don't need you to be... damaged

145

because you followed me."

"Damaged? I'm not going to be damaged. Will my life be different because I met you? Yes—that's already happened. But I want to live an adventure, not just watch them in movies."

I nodded absently, thinking how Evie's vision of me as a Human-Bigfoot ambassador brought even more dangers, how my father had died. "I don't think adventures are like the movies."

"Obviously. We just spent the whole day in a car. In a movie, that would have been a montage. Unfortunately, we had the glory of experiencing it."

I laughed, but it faded fast. I needed to explain myself better, and I met her gaze. "Evie just told me that the Fae's magic is weakening, and the boundary will fail. The Bigfoots need to meet humans, and she believes I can ease the transition."

Payton tilted her head. "Wow."

"Evie thinks I'm someone I'm not."

"Stop that! You've learned so much since I met you." She sighed and then laughed. "The day I met you, you didn't even know how to serve a volleyball."

"I still failed to protect Bryson."

"But you're here for him now, aren't you?"

I considered pointing out that Jaria and Evie were the ones talking with the Fae but knew she'd have a counterargument. While I'd made mistakes, I was working to correct them too.

"You'll need me," she added.

"As a friend? Definitely." A friend who stayed far away from danger.

"But I can be more than that." Payton paused. "I'm the first human to travel this far into Bigfoot land, right?" I nodded. "If you're to become this Bigfoot ambassador, maybe I can be the human envoy to the

146

Bigfoots?" She sat taller. "I'd like that."

"And I don't like it when people I care about take risks."

"Alice, you take risks every single time you set foot in Piner. I can choose for myself."

I glared at her, and she scowled back.

Then movement caught my attention. Maybe Evie and Payton were back with Bryson, and our wait was over—

But it was only a stag. The animal darted across the clearing, running like it had been startled.

I turned to Payton, prepared to deliver my newest rebuttal. But then I noticed a Bigfoot was rushing toward us, his face contorted in fear and fury.

Heron.

Chapter 24

Heron grabbed Payton before I could warn her, before I could reach her. He pulled her body to his chest, holding her like a prized hunting target.

She struggled, fighting with fists and elbows, but there was no competition. He was too big, too powerful.

"No!" I shouted.

I ran forward, closing the distance between us. I yanked at his paws, desperate to get them off Payton. He kicked out, landing a blow on my bad knee.

I tumbled to the ground, and he glowered over me.

"Now I see what you're plotting," he said. "You and Jaria are nothing but traitors. You help humans across the boundary and take them into our lands. You—witches."

"We work for the Fae! I can't expect you to understand."

"The Fae made the boundary. They wouldn't allow a human to cross it!" he roared.

"She's here to help..." I began, but then he shook Payton like a toy in his arms, and she whimpered. "Please don't hurt her."

"Her kind would destroy us if they had the chance."

"That's not true."

"What do you know of humans?"

"A lot more than you!"

He growled, preparing to strike me again.

"Heron, stop!" A new voice shouted, forcing me to hesitate. Daylen.

Hope fluttered in my chest. Daylen could best Heron in a fight; I'd seen him do it the other day—assuming Daylen would help.

Heron's grip on Payton slacked—not enough for her to wiggle free, but he was no longer hurting her.

Payton made eye contact with me and I held it, steadying my breath as she did the same. It was the best comfort we could offer each other.

"Daylen," I said, watching Payton's curiosity perk as I identified him. "Why are you here?"

"We're hunting." Daylen lifted a bow, and I noticed a quiver of arrows on his back.

"And good thing too," Heron said. "Otherwise no one would know about your wicked secrets. Now, Daylen, help me take this human to the village. Then everyone will know of your deceit."

I swallowed. Even as we prepared to introduce Bigfoots to humanity... My people remained terrified of humans. The fear had grown over the generations.

It was a belief that would have to change. But this would not accomplish that.

"What does he know?" I asked Daylen.

"Nothing," he replied.

Heron glared at Daylen. "Are you keeping secrets too?"

I glanced at the rabbit hole. Hopefully, Jaria and Evie would return soon. I didn't have the strength or experience to take Payton away from Heron. Instead, I had to convince him to let her go or persuade

Daylen to fight on her behalf.

Payton looked at me, impressively poised and calm, and her gaze steadied me.

I inhaled and began, "The boundary will fade. We've got time to prepare, but we can't continue to hide."

"Impossible," Heron growled. Even Daylen seemed uncomfortable. This was news to him too.

"It's scary, but the Fae have a plan. We're working on that, and Payton—the woman you're holding—is part of that plan."

Heron shuddered. "We can't! They'll destroy us. Come on Daylen, let's go."

Daylen didn't move.

"Fine," Heron spat. "I'll take her myself." He pulled Payton over his shoulder and began walking away.

I ran after him, reaching for Payton.

He turned and snarled at me.

"We're working on a solution," I said. "But if you parade a human around in the village, it will cause chaos."

"They deserve to know." He spat at the ground in front of me. "I can't believe you're betraying your own people."

His accusation hit harder than any kick. Appearing human was novel, but it wasn't who I was. I hadn't been raised as a human; I was Bigfoot.

"I'm going," Heron said. He shifted Payton and began jogging away.

Payton squirmed, pummeling her fists into his back, fighting with every step he took.

"Stop!" I yelled, chasing after him, inevitably slowed by my bad knee. "She's my friend."

"You shouldn't be friends with humans!" he

shouted back.

He kept running, and I couldn't catch up.

Still, I chased. I'd follow him all the way to the village if necessary. If I couldn't convince him, I needed to find someone he respected. Mother Gazina would help, maybe Pa—

Daylen brushed against my side, falling into pace beside me. He'd left the bow and arrows behind. "I can stop him."

I bit my lip, hating that I couldn't do this alone. "Please help."

He dashed ahead, racing to reach Heron. I followed as fast as I could, my eyes locked on Payton. She seemed so small flung over his back like that—

With a loud grunt, Daylen leaped and pulled Heron's free shoulder. Heron stumbled and stopped, but he didn't fall.

Heron turned to face Daylen. Payton used the opportunity to kick his chest. He threw her to the ground, and I gasped, begging my body to run faster.

Thankfully Payton sat up quickly, seemingly uninjured. She stood, but Heron had her trapped, blocked into a thorny thicket.

Heron lowered into a fighting stance and pivoted as Daylen circled him. It reminded me of their fight earlier—except this time, their claws were bared.

I reached them, lingering a few steps back. My heart pounded in my chest, not just from my run, but from fear. In a fight, I wouldn't have much advantage, but how did I use what I had?

Heron struck first, and Daylen dodged. Then Daylen swiped, and Heron ducked. They launched into a series of fast, furious blows.

I looked at Payton. She bounced on her heels, ready to spring at her first opportunity. I pointed to the left, hoping it communicated something of my plan, and she nodded.

Daylen drew first blood, slashing two of his claws against Heron's shoulder. Heron roared, brushing his hand against the bleeding wound.

Daylen stepped back, staring at his paw, stunned by what he'd just done.

And Heron leaped forward. He took full advantage of Daylen's distraction, kicking at Daylen's legs and punching at his face.

Daylen lost his footing and fell to the ground.

Heron took a step closer to Daylen, his gaze heated and locked in a rage so deep he appeared calm.

Daylen pressed his hands against the ground, preparing to stand—Heron kicked his shoulder. He forced Daylen back to the ground.

"I'm stronger than you, and I always will be," Heron said. "Submit and help me take this human to the village."

Daylen shook his head. "I can't do that."

Heron snarled, unfurling his claws anew. He prepared for another strike.

I gnashed my teeth and expanded my claws.

Payton jolted as I sprang into action.

I pushed Heron, ramming my momentum into his side. He brushed me off, barely shifting to stay upright.

I jumped away, hoping he'd choose to face me instead of chasing Payton. I couldn't take Heron in a direct fight, but if I was fast, I could run him in circles. As I had hoped—feared?—Heron turned to me.

He lunged forward, and I darted beyond his reach. He attacked a second time—I moved too slow. His fist struck my chest. I fell back, my butt slamming into the dirt.

The impact of my landing ricocheted through me, and my chest throbbed. I gasped, desperate to regain control of my body.

Heron took another step toward me, and I prepared to dodge by rolling to the side.

"Don't you dare!" Daylen shouted.

Heron twisted and reoriented his attack, striking Daylen instead of me.

Daylen tripped backward and fell. There was an awful *thunk*. His head banged into a tree, and he crumpled to the ground. He didn't get back up.

"No!" I cried, crawling closer to him. The sound of his landing reverberated in my ears. But he had to be all right, had to be, had to be…

I shook his arm, his leg, but he didn't stir.

Heron didn't stop me from reaching Daylen. "I didn't mean to…" Heron gasped. "Is he okay?"

I positioned my ear over Daylen's mouth, watching his chest. Holding my breath, I waited. A moment passed. Then I was certain that I felt the heat of his breath. That I saw the rise and fall of his chest.

"He's breathing," I said, hoping it would be enough.

"Good," Heron said.

I nodded my agreement. Hopefully, Daylen just needed time. This had shocked Heron, and maybe now we could talk—

My shoulder exploded with agony, and I gasped.

Heron pinched my forearm behind my back, pinning my shoulder at an awkward angle. He pulled me taught, and my vision narrowed with the pain.

He forced me to stand by lifting my arm. I twisted, faced him, and roared. Spittle sprayed from my mouth, speckling his face. I continued as long as there was breath in my lungs.

He wrapped me with his other arm, trapping me in his angry embrace. I shook, shifted, and twisted. But nothing broke his hold on me.

I couldn't fight my way out of this. It was time to change tactics.

"You don't want to do this," I told him. "There—"

The ground shook. The scents of magic and blood scorched the air, and an unseen force pulled us apart.

Chapter 25

I stirred, lying with my back against the ground. My eyes flitted open and closed. Clouds shifted in the murky sky as pine branches swayed in the wind...

"What are you doing?" Heron asked, his voice sounding far away.

Nobody responded to his question. But I heard a grunt.

I pressed myself into a sitting position, wobbling as my vision cleared. Earthy smells began overpowering those of magic and blood.

My gaze drifted to Heron.

Were those vines?

Heron was bound with thorny blackberry vines. They rose from the earth, wrapping his legs and wrists and forcing him to kneel. He thrashed but couldn't break the binding.

Jaria stood before him.

She had draped a few feet of vine around her wrist, tangling it with the cord of her crystal. Blood dripped from the vine.

Her palm had been cut. She still bled.

I shouldn't have been shocked. I'd seen Jaria use magic several times. But this? I'd never seen her do anything so... violent.

He looked up at Jaria and roared. She snarled and

clenched her fist in reply. The vines tightened around him.

They locked eyes, lost in their primal argument.

I looked past them to see Evie—and Bryson. My brother stood next to her, his eyes glazed and distant. He was singing to himself, Faerydust glittering on his skin. But at least he was there.

Payton glanced from them and to me. When nothing happened, she rushed to my side.

"You okay?" she asked.

My shoulder and knee ached, but nothing serious. "Yeah, I'll be all right. You?"

"I'm fine."

"Thank goodness." I stood, wobbled a step, and stilled.

Neither Jaria nor Heron had shifted.

My eyes wandered to Daylen. I studied him for another long moment, following his chest as it rose and fell. Intuitively, I stepped his direction, longing to tend to him—but there wasn't much I could do.

Instead, I forced myself to approach Heron and Jaria. They remained fixated upon each other, frozen in their battle of wills. Maybe Jaria needed help.

I reached for Jaria's free hand and held it. She was tense.

"You've got him," I said. "Thank you."

Without looking away from Heron, she squeezed my hand and then relaxed it with a sigh. She shifted the bewitched vine, and those around Heron loosened, just a little, while still binding him in place.

They resumed staring at each other.

I turned to Evie. She was comforting Bryson, who had burst into tears. He needed Payton's help. This was why she had come, wasn't it? I glanced to Daylen and grew impatient. It was time to do something.

"Heron, what will you do if Jaria releases you?" I asked.

He didn't respond at once. Jaria squeezed my hand again, but it was the only answer either of them gave.

The strangest thing about Heron was that, while I disliked him, I didn't hate him. I understood his need to question us and take Payton to the village. Despite her slight stature, her presence was a threat.

I knew how we were raised to think of humans: oppressive, destructive, and selfish. Generations of Bigfoots had reinforced the myth, supporting the idea that humans couldn't be trusted with our existence. Being trapped by humans had been my childhood nightmare.

I compared my former ideas of humans to what I knew now, finding the differences laughable. Humans weren't simply good or bad, and neither were Bigfoots.

But that was not common knowledge. Only a few of us understood how complex humanity was.

I couldn't blame Heron for reacting as he had. He thought he was protecting his village. From a particular perspective, his fight might even be noble.

Something shifted in the corner of my eye— Daylen was sitting up! My hand was still tangled with Jaria's, and I fought the urge to run to him.

"What would you do if Jaria releases you?" I repeated.

Heron finally replied, his gaze never leaving Jaria, "I don't believe in many things. The Fae are too mischievous for my taste. However," he paused, "I believe in strength."

Jaria tensed, and the vines tightened.

He looked at her. "And you are strong. I have

misjudged you, Jaria, apprentice to the Mother, and you have humbled me." He straightened his spine and announced, "It's my honor to keep this secret."

Jaria stiffened with consideration. Then she shifted, moving as if the vines around her wrist were a crown. Finally, she extended her bewitched hand and presented it to Heron. "Promise your silence with a kiss, and your vow can never be broken."

He reached out and tucked her bloody hand between his hands. He brought her fingers to his lips and, without ever breaking eye contact, kissed her palm.

Jaria gasped. The vines withered, disintegrating into air. She lifted her hands, helping him rise to his feet.

He stood over her. Jaria didn't back away, didn't back down. He bowed his head to his chest.

With a heavy nod, she withdrew her hand from his. "Help Daylen home," she instructed. "He needs water and rest, but don't let him sleep for several hours. Summon myself or Mother Gazina if his condition worsens."

"I will." Heron turned from her.

I dropped Jaria's hand and ran to Daylen, reaching him first.

Those moments we had shared in the fight—how I had fought to protect him, how he had taken a strike for me—our brief connection already felt like a dream.

And I was chasing the fantasy.

Quickly, I pressed my lips against his mouth. I darted back, treasuring the sweet taste of the stolen kiss.

Daylen chuckled as his mouth shifted to a giant grin. That smile told me a million things, but only one mattered: he still cared for me the way I cared for him.

Working together, Heron and I helped him stand. I lingered as he steadied onto his feet.

"Goodbye," I whispered as Heron and Daylen walked away.

Chapter 26

"By the Fae." I turned to Jaria as Heron and Daylen walked away. "That was amazing!"

Jaria looked at me, her shoulders hunching as they usually did. She crossed her arm over her chest, and her strength vanished.

Evie made a sound, like a click, and Jaria sighed. She closed her eyes and straightened her back. Her confidence shakily returned.

"You're so talented." I pulled Jaria into a hug.

She remained stiff in my arms.

I backed off, but she reached for my hand and held it. I cleared my throat and said, "I'll never understand what happened with the Fae. And I can't fix everything that's broken between us, but I'm ready to try."

"I'd like that." Jaria sniffed.

I turned to Evie and Bryson. Now my brother lay on his back, smiling peacefully at the sky.

"Is he okay?" I asked.

"This is... normal." Evie lowered herself, carefully settling beside him. "He's readjusting to our dimension, but Payton's presence can help ground him."

I sat nearby. Payton and Jaria sat such that we made a circle around Bryson. I reached out to stroke his face and was relieved when he nuzzled my palm.

"What do I need to do?" Payton asked.

"Touch his forehead with your thumb," Evie instructed.

She extended her hand.

Bryson startled when she was inches away. "Human!" he cried. He snapped his jaws and glared at her.

Payton yanked her hand away but didn't cower. "Your name is Bryson, right?" she asked.

"Yes."

"Alice has told me so much about you. I'm Payton. Maybe she's told you a little about me."

"She has." He tried to study her, but his gaze drifted away. He considered a bird that had settled on the circle of stumps.

I added, "Because Payton is human, she can make the Faerydust vanish. She journeyed a long way to help you."

His gaze drifted back to Payton. "No fur. Aren't you cold?"

"That's why humans wear clothes, silly." I reached out to bop him on the nose—but a flash of fear darted across his face, stopping me. "All Payton needs to do is touch your forehead. Can she do that?"

He gathered his brave face and nodded. But he also wiggled his fingertips forward and grabbed my knee.

"Go ahead," Evie said.

Payton brought her open palm closer to his furry face. He scrunched his eyebrows but didn't squirm. She haloed her hand over his head and settled her thumb on his forehead.

Glitter exploded everywhere.

Faerydust leaped from his fur, dissolving as it

contacted the air. Silver and gold and opalescent and magical—a force from a different world. I rubbed my itching nose.

Bryson sat up and turned to me, his eyes focused as they met mine. "Alice," he said, "you look exhausted."

"What?"

He chuckled, the sound a key to my heart. It wasn't the manic laughter he had made with the Fae. No, this was Bryson. I tugged him to me, and he snuggled into my chest. My brother, my baby brother, had returned.

"Don't ever follow me again," I whispered into his head, the request too quiet to be heard. He'd never agree to such a thing. Bryson was my brother, through and through.

He pulled back, turning to Payton. "You're really here." He looked at Evie and scrunched his brow. "And who are you?"

"I'm your..." She searched for a word. "I'm Alice's ma."

"You're my stepma?"

"You can call me Evie."

"You can be my stepma," Bryson said with sudden seriousness. "I used to be jealous that Alice had both a ma and a stepma. Having an extra mom sounds nice."

Evie looked at me quizzically. I shrugged, knowing my family would have to discuss this later. Once I'd brought Evie to them...

A droplet of rain splashed on my hand, and I turned to the darkening sky.

"We should go," Jaria said.

Sunset. I searched for the sun but couldn't find it behind the clouds. Maybe, if I ran fast enough, I could make it.

"I need to go," I realized.

"Go where? Now?" Jaria asked.

But Payton gasped. Her voice grew shrill. "Sunset on Friday! Alice has a date with Mark!" She clapped her hands.

"Who's Mark?" Evie asked.

I gaped at her, trying to figure out how to clarify, and then remembered she'd seen me kiss Daylen. *I'd kissed Daylen!* "I'll explain later."

"I'll help Payton home," Jaria offered. "And Evie can take Bryson to the village. Mother Gazina should see him first."

Evie looked at me. "I can do that, if it's okay with both of you."

This arrangement meant I wouldn't be there when everyone was reunited. Bryson and Evie with Stepma and Pa. I'd been curious to watch, to observe their relationships. But maybe some things were best handled by the adults.

"I like Evie," Bryson said. "And I know you like Mark. You should go on this date."

"I like Evie too," I admitted, and she smiled at me. "Tell Stepma and Pa that I'll be home soon."

Evie nodded, and I looked to the darkening sky.

"Go," Payton said. "I'll see you Monday morning?"

I nodded, but still, I hesitated. It was strange to leave Payton in Jaria's care.

"We'll be okay," Jaria added. "I can protect her."

"Of course you can." I turned on my heels and ran.

Chapter 27

My knee ached as I took my first few steps, but the stiffness subsided as the joint warmed up. I settled into the rhythm of my pace and raced to meet Mark.

The sun would certainly set before I would get there.

But even if I was running on time, would he be there? Payton had become nervous near the perimeter. Mark had approached before, but I didn't understand how the boundary worked. Would he be able to near it today?

I pushed onward, driving myself forward. Bryson was right, I was exhausted. Regardless, I focused on the task at hand. One step at a time, every single one driving me closer to my destination.

More droplets of rain struck me. But while the clouds continued to darken, they stifled their pending downpour.

My mind grew hazy, but I trusted the flow of my body as I ran. I recalled the day I'd met Mark, on Summer Solstice. He hadn't even known I was there, but I'd watched him through the boundary. He was the first human I'd ever seen, and from that moment, I'd longed to meet him.

It also felt like I barely knew him. We rarely

crossed paths outside of school, and yet, we started every single school day together. We had developed something between us. Or at least I believed we had. And I longed to explore that something further.

Even if I'd kissed Daylen.

I couldn't grasp why I'd done it, but I didn't regret it. No, it worried me because of what it meant. I still had feelings for Daylen, feelings I didn't intend to act upon.

Still, I ran toward Mark.

Finally, I crested the last hill and reached the fallen tree. No one was there. I jumped onto the trunk and leaped across the perimeter, landing in my human form on the other side wearing a raincoat over jeans and matching boots. Whatever magic controlled my clothing choices had fine taste.

"Mark!" I called out.

Nothing.

I ran forward, looking for movement. It was dusk and becoming difficult to see—if I went to the house, I could find a flashlight. I started walking toward the narrow stream.

"Mark!" I cried again.

"Alice? I'm here!" Mark's voice was distant. "Sorry I'm running late! I couldn't find the spot!"

"What?" I asked, wondering again how the boundary worked. It seemed as temperamental as an intelligent being.

"Where are you?" he asked.

I held my breath, letting my lungs burn while I listened, searching for sounds of him stomping on leaves or cracking branches.

There.

I raced further down the stream, adrenaline pushing my exhausted body onward.

"Where are you?" he asked, and I knew I wasn't far.

"I'm nearly there!" I reached a ledge where the stream turned into a short waterfall.

He stood below, dressed in an oversized raincoat and thankfully carrying a lantern. I froze, relieved that we had actually found each other in the twilight.

"It's easier to cross down there." I pointed to a grouping of boulders not far away. I prepared to descend.

But before I began, he clipped the lantern to his backpack and began scampering up the rocks. His shoe slipped on the moss, but he didn't fall.

I leaned over and offered him my hand. He took it, and I marveled at his human touch. Flesh touching flesh had bothered me once, but there was a warmth to it that I'd grown to appreciate.

Mark reached the top and released my grip. He shifted the pack on his back.

"Thanks for sticking around," he said. "I guess the trees look different at dusk... I'm sorry I kept you waiting."

"Actually, I'm running late too. More family drama." The honesty surprised me; it would have been easy to hide my tardiness. "So, I'm sorry too!"

He laughed. "This is ridiculous. I tried to do something sweet, but it didn't go according to plan. But somehow, we both made it here."

"We made it," I agreed, but my smile turned sour. Until that moment, I had been so worried about finding him that I'd forgotten how upset I'd been at the movies—

"Who was that girl?" I blurted out.

He looked puzzled. "What girl?"

"What girl!" I spat and, realizing my tone, began

calming myself down. "At the movie theater. I know we're not together or anything—but I didn't realize you were seeing anyone else..."

He looked confused, and then his eyes grew wide with realization. "You thought I was on a date with Macey?" Now he looked horrified. "She's my cousin! Is that why you ran into the bathroom?"

"Oh." My concern lingered, but I had no reason to doubt him. "Well, that's a relief."

"I didn't even realize how you might've seen that." He shook his head.

A drop of water landed on my shoulder, and a second one fell on my hand. I heard the clicks of more raindrops falling around us, accelerating in tempo. The rain had come.

I scanned our surroundings. Several bushes grew together, and they formed a shelter. It would be too short to stand, but we could sit.

"Let's get some cover." I pointed toward the thicket. "Shame it's raining."

"I don't mind," he replied. "Umm, I brought a blanket? Maybe that'll help."

He pulled it from his pack, and working closely, we spread it over the low space. It began to pour, but we stayed dry.

We sat side by side, our legs inches from each other. The pitter-patter of rain covered our silence.

"So much for spring break," I said. "It's still cold and rainy."

"But you've seen the flower buds? And now the sun rises before school starts."

"Yes—and maybe I'm greedy—but I wanted more. Flowers and blue skies. Look at us!" I laughed. "We're hiding under a bush from the rain!"

"But Alice..." When he didn't continue, I worried

my complaining had scared him off, but eventually he swallowed and continued, "I know this isn't our prettiest scene, but it's real—it's ours. Despite everything, we found each other, and that makes this moment exceptional."

His words made me smile. I longed to tell him everything, wondering how he'd respond if I actually explained my life. I wanted to know what insight he might have. I wish he could tell me his thoughts on Evie or if I had worried too much about Payton.

Mark had the uncanny ability to cut to the heart of the matter. And in that moment, it seemed impossible for me to absorb everything that had happened.

"I'm not exactly in the best headspace tonight," I said. "All the family drama... it's been difficult."

He laughed. "It happens."

"So maybe we should meet another night—" I shifted forward, ready to leave the brambles behind.

"But first, I brought food."

Food? He knew the way to my heart.

"Just hot chocolate and cookies," he added. "Nothing too fancy."

"It sounds wonderful." I settled next to him.

He pulled a thermos and two mugs from his pack. Then he brought out a package of chocolate chip cookies. He poured the hot chocolate and handed me a mug.

But before I took my first sip—he dunked his cookie into my drink.

"Gross!" I pushed his hand away.

He laughed, tossing the cookie into his mouth. "You can dip your cookie in my drink. Fair is fair."

"Okay." I daintily dipped my cookie in his hot chocolate.

"You don't need to explain what happened, but I'll sit with you if that helps."

"I want to tell you Mark, I really do." I nibbled the cookie and swallowed. "But I'm not ready."

"That's okay." He leaned over and kissed my cheek.

I didn't dodge away, but I couldn't ask for more. Instead, I leaned against him, resting my head against his shoulder. And after a moment's hesitation, he wrapped his arm around me.

I'm not sure how long we stayed that way, sharing food and listening to the rain. But it was long enough for my mind to slow its spinning.

Chapter 28

My outer fur was covered in rainwater by the time I reached my family's cabin. Mark and I had separated as dusk turned to dark night. We had talked little, instead sharing a silence and a deep lingering hug.

Despite the lack of banter or passion, I felt secure. The fresh memories of my thicket picnic with Mark kept me warm on the damp walk home.

Noisy chatter escaped the cabin's door with a mixture of many voices. I smelled a meaty stew. Steeling myself under the deck's covering, I shook the water from my fur before opening the door.

The fire burned hotter and brighter than normal, the way Stepma kept it for a holiday. The stew was only the beginning of the food. I saw candied nuts, rolls with apple butter, and even a bottle of mead. Stepma must have dug into her hidden stores.

It was a night for celebrating.

"Alice!" Stepma ran forward. She swept a blanket from the back of a chair and wrapped it around my shoulders. "You're so wet!"

She pulled a chair before the fire and practically pushed me into it. She forced a bowl of hot soup into one of my hands and a mug of tea into the other.

"Eat," she commanded.

Usually, I'd shove her away and tell her she was

overbearing. But tonight, I didn't mind. My body was exhausted, and I longed to sit.

I scanned the room and saw Evie and Pa sitting at the dinner table with a set of dice between them. They continued their game as Stepma fussed over me, each of them knowing it was best to give me a moment. The evidence of their friendship seemed both strange and familiar. Catching Evie's eye, I smiled.

Jaria sat with her back against the wall. Bryson was asleep in her lap, and I imagined him drifting to sleep as he questioned her on the Fae. He'd pick her brain for every piece of information she'd accidentally give.

Stepma pulled up a chair beside me. "How did it go with Mark?"

"Stepma!" I looked at my soup. "Fine. Okay, maybe even good."

"Did you kiss him?"

"No!"

"Evie said you kissed Daylen."

I grumbled, acknowledging the truth of it. The fire crackled and sparked, and I turned to the dancing flames. Light flickered on the walls, warming the cabin. "I really like him," I said. "Mark, I mean. I had a hard time talking tonight—but being around him was nice."

"You can be yourself with him."

"Yes, but how is that possible? I'm definitely not myself." Then again, my Bigfoot identity wasn't as real as I'd assumed. "I can't exactly tell him the truth. 'Hi, I'm actually a Bigfoot—well, half-Bigfoot.'"

She laughed at my forced joke. Good. "Maybe he just knows you as Alice, whoever you are regardless of which appearance you're wearing."

I lifted the crystal pendant from my chest, turning it in the firelight, studying the way it captured its glow. It was hard to believe the Fae had bewitched it when I was born.

It separated me, divided me into two. But it gave me the freedom to blend into either society, providing me with the opportunity to fit in before I discovered I was different.

"Thanks for..." I failed to meet her eyes and studied her lips instead. "Everything."

"Of course." She took my empty bowl. "Now, can you do me a favor?"

"Anything."

"Tuck Bryson into bed. I promised him he could stay awake until you were home."

It was one chore I wouldn't mind.

Jaria looked at me with relief as I settled down beside them. I stroke Bryson's arm and smiled as he stirred.

"You fell asleep," I accused.

"Did not!" He sat up defiantly, and despite his efforts to hold it back, he yawned.

"I'll tuck you in, come on." I began climbing the ladder into our bedroom loft.

He turned to Jaria. "One last question. When can I visit the Fae again? And if you won't take me, I'll climb in there myself and—"

"What did I say about asking permission?" Jaria interrupted.

"The Fae Queen prefers guests, not intruders," he recited. "But will you help me?"

"If both Queen Avilana and your parents agree, I could use your company during the next full moon."

He wiggled with excitement and yawned again.

"Let's go, sleepyhead," I called down from the loft.

He scampered up and jumped into his bed. "While I was with the Fae, I learned about making deals."

"What did you learn?"

"When you want something, you make a deal. I want something from you."

"What's that?" I pulled the blanket to his chin.

"I want you to stay in the Bigfoot Village one day a week. No going to Piner or Jaria's house. Be here with us."

The request sounded simple, something that shouldn't make me hesitate. After everything I'd put him through, I wanted to promise him anything. But the words didn't come freely.

When had staying in the village become difficult? When had I changed? It was hard to know. But I had to find a way to straddle my two different worlds. I needed to belong to both.

This was a deal that I needed to make. Not just for Bryson but myself. I agreed, "From here on out, I promise to stay in the village one day a week."

"That's not a proper Fae deal, but I accept."

"Good, because I'm not making any deals with you. I don't want to know what tricks you learned from the Fae."

He smiled mischievously and yawned again.

"Go to sleep." I kissed his forehead.

I retreated to my bed, debating if I wanted to be alone, but I heard the tumble of dominos. Peering over the loft's edge, I saw Stepma, Pa, Evie, and Jaria crowded around the table. There was room for one more.

I scrambled down the ladder to join my family.

Epilogue

I rose earlier than normal the following Monday morning. Despite resting all weekend, my knee was still swollen, and Stepma made me promise not to run for a week. It was good advice, even if I had stuck my tongue out when she had given it.

Bryson continued to sleep. I blew him a kiss and descended the ladder. No matter what else happened, he would always be my baby brother.

Pa was sitting at the table in his typical chair with his typical glass of water. He silently ate the jerky and nuts in his bowl.

He grunted in acknowledgment, and I grumbled a reply. I grabbed my breakfast and sat beside him.

"I'm sorry," he blurted.

I whipped my head to look at him. "I can't blame you for not telling me everything—"

He waved his hand dismissively. "It's not that."

I waited.

"I haven't been the most supportive of your new role."

"You've been trying to protect me—"

"Let me speak."

I nodded, apprehensive. His fingers were fidgeting. As much as I valued his support, this sudden uncertainty caught me by surprise.

He continued, "I had my own biases when I raised you. I wanted you to fit in, to belong, and maybe... maybe I've pushed too hard. I was afraid you'd be left out, and now I'm wondering if I should have encouraged you to become who you needed to be."

I took a long drink of water as I sifted through his words. Swallowing, I replied, "Thanks to you, I know what it means to be Bigfoot. I had the chance to grow up normal. And I appreciate that."

That made him smile. He sat back in his chair and bit into his jerky.

We left the cabin together. "No running," he reminded me as we went our separate ways.

Walking meant the journey to the perimeter took forever, but it gave my thoughts time to wander. This was my first departure from the Bigfoot Village since Friday, making it the longest I'd stayed since... I couldn't remember how long.

The rain had continued through the weekend, but the Monday morning sky was clear. The sun rose with brilliant colors, promising to dry the earth. The air carried a fresh scent, carrying life into my lungs.

Spring.

I'd forgotten what that felt like. For a moment, everything was right with the world. I was exactly where I was supposed to be.

I reached the house with an extra skip in my step, but I stopped in my tracks the moment I saw the building. The yard looked strange.

Stones outlined a large rectangle along one edge of the building. Tall branches stood like posts at regular intervals, spiders knitting a thick web between the sticks.

The scent of magic itched at my nose, and I walked the long way around to reach the front door.

Still, I smiled. Evie's new suite was already under construction.

"Morning," I said as I stepped into the house. "I'm headed to school. Jaria, are you going in to town today?"

Evie and Jaria sat on the couch. Both seemed half-asleep.

"Not today." Jaria rose to her feet. "I should go to bed."

"Did you work all night?" I asked.

"Moonlight is the best for spells..." Evie stretched out on the couch, claiming the space Jaria had vacated.

"Do you need anything while I'm out?"

"Coffee," Evie said. "I love you. Not just for coffee. But that you cared to ask."

"I love you too," I admitted, the words surprising me. It was hard to understand everything I felt toward Evie, but I knew there was love.

I glanced at the stack of non-fiction books on the desk. They were as daunting as before, but now I understood why I needed them. "I love both of you for many different reasons."

The school gym was the loudest it had been in months. While my teammates lingered around the nets, they fiddled with the ball and rarely volleyed. Everyone was more interested in talking than playing.

I listened as the others recounted their adventures, avoiding any situation where I'd need to explain mine. If I heard enough of their stories, I could construct my own.

Soon, Payton arrived, and I ran from the court, missing a ball I could have returned. But I hadn't seen her since Friday. "Jaria told me you're fine, but I'm so glad to see you!"

She hugged me tight. "Jaria texted me, said you were staying in the village. Is Bryson okay?"

"Yes, thanks so much for your help," I stepped back, examining her at arm's length. "What about you, after Heron... I'm so sorry—"

"Alice, look at me."

I did.

Payton continued, "What you're doing is important, but it's also dangerous." This was exactly what I hoped she would realize. This wasn't a movie; this wasn't fun and games.

"If you want out, I understand," I replied. "Maybe Jaria can develop a more complex memory spell and—"

"I don't want out," she said. "I want to be more involved."

"But it's dangerous—"

"Jaria already has ideas for how I can help."

And to think, I had hoped bringing Jaria and Payton together would be a good thing.

"You can't be the only one taking risks," Payton added.

The bell rang for homeroom.

"I'm not going to be able to change your mind, am I?" I asked.

"I wouldn't bet on it."

I sighed. But it wouldn't be all bad. Once I stopped fearing for Payton's safety, it would be nice to have her around. "You're right, by the way."

"I'm right about what? Everything?"

I laughed. "You're right that we should start a

blog."

"That?" She shook her head. "Well, I guess it's good to have a hobby. Maybe we can start with *Goblins*. We could see it again this weekend and—"

"Payton," Lexi called as we started walking from the gym. "I guess you didn't have time to go shopping over the break. Too busy working?"

Payton was wearing another shirt from Fresher Food Market. This one featured fruits and vegetables as cartoons.

Payton pulled a bag of cookies from her backpack. "These were baked yesterday, but they're still really good. Enjoy!"

She shoved them into Lexi's hands and walked away. I chased after her.

"Why did you give her cookies?" I whispered.

She shrugged. "It worked on Jaria."

We were walking up the stairs when she asked, "So tell me about your date with Mark."

"Honestly, I had a hard time opening up. I was still a little off after everything that happened. But he was nice about that."

"What about Daylen? Jaria said he was recovering okay."

"He is." I'd visited Daylen with Stepma. She had done most of the talking while Daylen and I avoided actual interaction. "But it's not like I could date him."

"Because of the whole Bigfoot suitorship thing?"

"Exactly." Although, if Daylen and I really wanted to be together, maybe we could probably find a way. Pa had already offered to help, but it would require a commitment that I wasn't ready for.

"Can you tell him thanks for his help?" Payton asked as we took our separate ways.

"Of course."

I walked toward my homeroom and froze outside the door. Mark was already at his seat, and I was eager to talk to him.

"Excuse me," a classmate pushed past me to enter the room. I couldn't just stand there.

So, I marched up to Mark and towered over his desk. This had to be my worst angle, but it also felt true. I *was* tall, and this was me.

"I'm not sure how I'm supposed to do this," I said, "but can we go on a proper date?" Suddenly, I was talking very fast. "I know *Goblins* wasn't your thing, but what sort of movies do you like? Or books?"

He looked up at me, his bright blue eyes filled with intrigue. "I'm a little more into documentaries."

I made a sour face and fell into my chair.

"Don't worry! I've got some in mind that are pretty exciting."

I faced my desk to discover there was a daffodil on it. It was the first I'd seen all season. It wasn't picture perfect but wild and vibrant.

Mark explained, "I saw it this morning. I feel a little bad about picking it, but I wanted to show you spring was here."

"Thank you." I ran my finger along a petal.

The bell rang, and Coach Higgins called for silence. "Welcome back. For attendance this morning, I want everyone to share one thing you did over break."

Many of my classmates groaned. But I studied my flower and began considering how I'd answer the question.

❧ ✿ ☙

Continue Alice's Adventure in
A Bigfoot's Destiny

Since spring break, Alice has struggled with her new identity. She believes she is a monster, but there is no time for self-pity, not when the Bigfoot's protective boundary is threatening to fail.

Meanwhile, Daylen prepares to pick a new Bigfoot suitor, Mark pressures Alice to tell him the truth, and Payton wants to be more involved, putting herself in danger.

Alice is already pushed to her limits when catastrophe strikes.

Forced into her truebody, Alice must accept her new identity. Completing this quest will require all her courage. It will test all of her relationships, even the one she has with herself.

Hopefully she can do this one thing right—the future of the Bigfoots depends on her.

Author's Note

Well then—that's a wrap for Bigfoot's Quest! Completing this book was an unexpectedly long journey, and it's surreal to be writing this note.

Like Alice might see this story, I'd best describe this manuscript as "nothing went according to plan." Side projects proved to be distractions (specifically The Wild Mermaid) and my day-to-day life transformed in light of the pandemic. Meanwhile, my original synopsis for this novel had to be thrown out the window the day both Alice and I discovered Evie had been at SEA willingly.

Plot-twists happen and side quests slow things down. Life is a wild ride, but this journey shapes me into whoever I'm becoming.

Thanks to my husband Josh for all his support. To Mark and Suzanne for their thoughts on the beta draft. And finally, Deanne for final read and edits.

Mel Braxton

About the Author

Mel lives in Portland, OR, where she daydreams of fantastical worlds and those who live there. She is an avid reader, lover of music, and passionate scientist. Lulu, her dog, mistakenly believes Mel's job is to be a professional puppy cuddler.

Made in the USA
Monee, IL
12 November 2021